Advance Praise for

All Things Are Labor

"In the lineage of Tillie Olsen and Diane Di Prima, Katherine Arnoldi
writes with revolutionary honesty and deep love. Her characters are
working class, are mothers, are artists, are people like you and me—
people turning our backs on the fear and obedience we have been
taught—people too rarely honored in literature. All Things Are Labor is
a book that renews faith in art, a book that makes you want to live a
better life, a masterpiece."
    —Ariel Gore, author of The Traveling Death and Resurrection Show: A Novel

"In Katherine Arnoldi's stories, girls are on the loose, long before
they're women, and labor is what they do . . . wherever, whenever.
These girls are unwed when it's uncool, they're digging, they're cutting
in, carrying on, running around, they're on the move, street to street,
New York City to Utah, in and out of order, they disrupt, they sweet-talk,
they're ready for anything, ready to hit you over the head with a chair if
that's what it takes. Better yet, when the women in Arnoldi's fiction have
visions, they're big, loud, and smelly. What more could you want from
this fast-paced insider look at outsiders."
    —Janet Kauffman, author of Collaborators: A Novel

"Brilliantly mesmerizing voices emerge with revelatory force from
Katherine Arnoldi's All Things Are Labor. Often single mothers, her characters engage in difficult, creative, finally heroic struggles to construct
lives of worth for themselves and their children. From the gritty (My Lot)
to the visionary (Journal Found in a Field), these crafty, laconic, compel-
ling narratives are triumphs of both the imagination and the spirit."
    —Jeff Gundy, author of Walker in the Fog: On Mennonite Writing

"How often might one remark of a work of fiction that there is not a
frivolous, underconsidered word to be found anywhere within it? All
Things Are Labor offers just such an occasion. Katherine Arnoldi's alertly
observed, gravely precise stories are giving and bravely original and wise.
To read them is to be smitten, enlarged, graced."
    —Gary Lutz, author of I Looked Alive: Stories

Kimmie,
Thanks so much for
your good words, your
spirit! Katherine
Arnoldi

ALL THINGS ARE LABOR

All Things Are Labor

Stories

Katherine Arnoldi

University of Massachusetts Press Amherst

This is a work of fiction, and any resemblance to persons
living or dead is coincidental.

LC 2007007354
ISBN 978-1-55849-603-3

Designed by Kristina Kachele Design, llc
Set in Quadraat with Insignia display
Printed and bound by The Maple-Vail Book Manufacturing Group

Library of Congress Cataloging-in-Publication Data
Arnoldi, Katherine.
All things are labor : stories / Katherine Arnoldi.
    p. cm.
ISBN 978-1-55849-603-3 (pbk. : alk. paper)
I. Title.
PS3601.R5854 79 2007
813'.6—dc22
            2007007354

British Library Cataloguing in Publication data are available.

Acknowledgments

For assistance and support thanks to the Michael Tuck Foundation; the DeJur Award; the Henfield TransAtlantic Fiction Award; the New York Foundation for the Arts; the MacDowell Colony; the Blue Mountain Center; the Hedgebrook Center for Women Writers, the William Flanagan Center, and Edward Albee; the City College of New York; the Newhouse Award; Binghamton University; the Nuyorican Poets Café; A Gathering of the Tribes; the Manhattan Mennonite Fellowship; the First Church of the Brethren (Canton, Ohio); and Camp Zion.

For support, inspiration and encouragement, thanks to Tillie Olsen, Steve Cannon, Jennifer Hengen, Neeti Madan, Sterling Lord, Bruce Wilcox, Jaime Colbert, Leslie Heywood, Fred Tuten, Mark Mirsky, Enid Mastrianni, Gloria Dialectic, Dr. Gerald Turino, Dr. Baron, Dr. Kahn, Fred Walsh, Jim Reidy, Jim Kellough, Peter Young, Eve Adesso, Wendy Rolnick, Kimberly Windbiel, Mary Ellen Callahan, Carol Betsch, Jameel Moondoc, Butch Morris, Mia Hansford, Jimmy Stewart, Tom Ross, Thom Corn, Amber, Dawn Raffel, Bob Schechter, Merry Fortune, Ellen Raskin, Eva Pekarkova, Neil Smith, Sabrina Jones, Terese Svoboda, Adele Heyman, Jane Kolber, Pam Blount, Djoniba, Bob Ward, the Weisses, John Ranard, Jim Feast, Richard Barcia, Jane Millwee, Sheryl Branham, Rose Conforti, Rena Cohen, Kathleen White, Howard Fireheart, Deborah Meade, Gloria Marquardt, Susie Wallace Mizer, Debbie Thomas, the Feemsters, and all in Gordon Lish's class.

The following stories have appeared in the following publications: "Seventeen" in Room of One's Own 18:1 (1995); "M" in The World 51 (1995); "X" in Fiction 12 (1994); "All Things Are Labor" in The Quarterly 25 (1993); "Ma Ripple" in ONTHEBUS 13 (1993); "Yonder's Wall" in New Observations 82 (1992); "Our Landlord" in Gathering of the Tribes 1:1 (1991); "Canton, Ohio" in The Quarterly 18 (1991); "Webfoot" in The Quarterly 14 (1990), "Crosscut Saw" in The Quarterly 15 (1990); "To Q from Linda Vitale" as "How I Became a Single Parent by Linda Vitale" in The Quarterly 12 (1989).

In gratitude to
Gordon Lish, my teacher

And for
the light I find in front, Stacie, my thin-boned child

Contents

ALL THINGS ARE LABOR

Crosscut Saw

All this is silent.

Sixty-seven people dressed in black walk single file through a field of snow. The sky is overcast, white. It should be someplace like Kansas, so it can be flat with no horizon. The people curlicue through the field of snow and stop at the side of a lake where a bus overturned a few hours before. They stare at a hole in the ice. A blue diaper bag pops to the surface and someone lifts it and sloshes it onto the ice. Then a watermelon bobs to the surface. Someone stoops, lifts the watermelon, and, cradling it in both hands, leads the sixty-seven people, all dressed in black, single file through the field of snow and back to the town.

I don't live in Kansas. I live on Avenue C in New York City. The rest of this is noisy.

My ex-lover told stories better than any of yours.

My ex-lover has brown eyes with a blue ring around the edge and he sees two ways, between and through, and has three ways of being, depending on the drug. In 1964 he dyed his hair silver to match his guitar, but just before a gig it all fell out, and that was his story.

My friend Anna senses things through her feet. Once, when we were standing in front of the Second Avenue Deli, she told me that her lover had stood in that exact spot an hour before kissing a new lover, and she was right, because I was across the street and saw it all.

"So what?" I said, "That's a pointless waste of good feet. Why can't you tell fortunes or something useful?" Two days later, when we were bringing back shrimp fried rice from Hop Fat's, she stopped in the middle of Avenue C, backed up a few steps, and told my future up until March 21, 2016, and everything has come true so far.

My ex-lover was strong and good. Once he jumped off a cliff and fell chest-first through the air and then glided into a river without a ripple.

I have just told a lie. My ex-lover was fifty, has emphysema, and brown, gutted teeth. He is weak and frail. He passed out every night.

"Do your teeth hurt?" I asked him once, when he brought them up.

"Hell, no," he said. "If one hurts, I get it taken out."

The people in the field were Mennonite, which explains their dress. I myself am Mennonite and this year planned to be at the foot-washing ceremony, but instead stayed home to be by the phone.

"He won't call," Anna says.

"Is that from your feet or your head?" I say.

"My feet."

"Damn," I say.

My ex-lover sang, "I'm a crosscut saw. Honey, drag me cross your log. I'll cut your wood so easy, can't help but say hot dog," but, as I already mentioned, he passed out every night.

I have just told another lie. My ex-lover could stay up all night, every night.

The Mennonite foot-washing ceremony goes like this: the women get up from the church pews and go to the basement. We sit in rows of folding chairs. The first woman in a row squats on her knees and washes the next woman's feet. She uses Ivory soap and dries the feet with a towel. Then both women stand, embrace, and kiss each other. Nobody talks until all the feet are washed.

My ex-lover sang about evil in your home, staying high all the time, do-wang-wang doodling all night, and going back to get his old gal Sue. His baby's long. His baby's tall. When she lays down in the kitchen, her feets stick way out in the hall.

I'm long and tall.

My great-grandmother was a doctor in Ohio and she traveled alone to Illinois to live with the Chippewa and improve her art. There she married a Chippewa man and brought him back to her Mennonite community. She was at someone's bedside when she looked up and said, "My husband just died. I have to go home."

"I want a VCR," my ex-lover said one morning. Within an hour, he named thirteen things he wanted. A turntable. A van. A new hat. His five-month-old child, who was taken away from the mother and put in foster care because he was born with a cocaine dependency. A new suit. A set of wineglasses. A new kitchen table. "This one rocks," he said.

Every Thursday we would go the Social Services center and the foster parent would bring the child to our cubicle for an hour. "He cries all night. Nothing but fussing with this one here," the foster parent would say.

It's February, cold. My ex-lover and I stand on Avenue A. A bowlegged person comes at us holding up what looks like an old dryer hose attached to a smashed electrical apparatus. "I came by it on a fluke," he says to us. "I came by it on a fluke," he says to the heavens. "I came by it on a fluke," he says over and over down Third Street.
"I came by everything the same way," my ex-lover says, and kisses me.

Then the mother of the child got out of jail.

"You two get married, get the child," I said, and packed every-thing in a Glad trash bag. My robe. My quilt. The box of Lipton tea I'd bought. "You owe me forty-three back rubs," I said.

"Could we make that forty-four?" he said.

Anna and I are thirty-seven. I draw hearts with fake valves and knees with plastic parts for medical publications. Anna makes hats and word-processes. For fifteen years we have been like this. As though we are lying on moss-covered rocks in a creek shaded by willow and sycamore trees. As though we have our feet together and heads cushioned on opposite banks. As though we've watched our lovers pass over our bodies like water and float downstream, far under the horizon.

Arline

From the first there were dances on Saturday night and feet to be washed on Sunday. There was gold to be mined from tree bark and a dog to stand in the water. There were men being dragged through doors, clothes without buttons, and an Arline at the bottom of skirts.

Arline hits a stick on fence posts until the sky turns red and still it is Snyders. Where one ends, the other begins. Underneath the earth is black, the richest, except for the Amish, but the Amish is not the direction Arline is headed.

Arline dreams of dances in the city, satin, and a dog on a leash. She dreams of taking off her gloves one finger at a time, being called on and standing up, wearing a color not black, giving the right answer, and, at the end, the procession of four-cornered hats. Then it would be Arline who feels a tap on her shoulder, a sweeping out to the center of the floor and a coming back to the table. Her lips would be red and bated.

Arline was dunked three times in a pool behind the pulpit. After that, there is no turning back.

Arline runs and runs and still is at the door, her door. The women hay and hoe and fill the bags of feed. They sweep out barns, scrub floors on their hands and knees, make blankets out of rags, feed four, then eight, then twelve on steaming bowls of corn, things in vinegar, stringy meat.

Arline digs into bark and pulls out gold. She mixes it with mud, makes cake. She digs worms in cans for her brothers Emerson and Robert. She goes to school, memorizes each poet, every Greek. She learns to wear a prayer cap like we Mennonites do. She learns to sew, to not get caught, to see in nothing the abundant, in the abundant, nothing. She learns to spit, to walk and to keep walking, and to not go back.

After the dunking, in truth quite brutal, Arline is allowed to wash the feet, to eat the bread, to call herself a Mennonite, work. There is work to do in Africa, South America, for the underground and overground railroads. There is a Bowery and a Tenderloin for a Mennonite who is young, who wants to see the world, who wants to be of service but that is not the world that Arline is looking at, that she can see. Instead Arline is looking at the worldly. Arline wants to be the first one who flies across the ocean, who gets out of her plane, raises her goggles and waves to a crowd, if only someone had not done it first. She wants to be the one in the photograph of a café in Paris, the one in the long black gloves, with a glass in her hand, looking up at the camera. There is jazz, improvisation, lipstick, the unconscious, even, perhaps a string of pearls. She wants to be the one who knows that poet, who has seen that painting, who has heard that composer, the one who is moved the most, who has gone the farthest to see what is ahead, the one who does not look back.

The life of the party pressed into her, the sweet Arline. He turned her around and around on a Saturday night, touched her thin waist, the nape of her neck. The life of the party knows how to sweep something as delicate as Arline out to the center and back. He knows how to move fast, to jump up on a vat and pour molten steel, to shovel coal if need be while he is waiting for a chance to use his good looks to sell people something, anything. And he can do it. He knows how to make sure everyone has a good time. He is from the world, from somewhere else, across the ocean, from Denmark. On the balcony his arm swoops out across the tops of trees, across the roofs, toward where a horizon might be; up to where, if this were somewhere else, are stars. All the roads have arrows that point to him, to the life of the party. All the eyes in every room look at the life of the party, at his perfect suit, his shoes, his cuffs, his hat.

Arline looks up at the life of the party, then out. She sees things beyond the ends of his fingers, things she could touch, places she could go, people she could meet. Arline says yes, then yes again to the life of the party. She has her eyes on the life of the party. She has her eyes on going out.

Out is not the direction Arline is going. The life of the party is for going out. Arline is for staying in the house, for writing down recipes, for cleaning edges of toilets, floors. She is for lightening up, putting her face back on right, for smoothing out her hair, for smiling, for making it look perfect.

Arline and the life of the party have a dog, like the one on TV, all hairy and ready to save lives, if only he were not chained out back. He is not a dog that likes a leash. His water bowl is a chunk of ice. He eats scraps from the table. At night he howls.

Arline brings babies home from the hospital, puts them in cribs, says, "I will not," and does not. They cry and cry but Arline is listening for feet on the steps. She is looking out over the rooftops, between the trees, down the streets. Arline is watching the life of the party for a sign, for a change, for something to be wrong. Arline is waiting for the clock to be the right time.

Arline wants the life of the party to dance with her on the oak floor, to take her out where someone can see her small waist, her long neck. She wants some new shoes, to sit at the table, to be the one that everyone is looking at, then to turn and to talk.

The life of the party does not.

Arline does not want to go back. She does not want to be at the bottom of skirts, to cook any corn, wash any floor. What she wants is something ahead.

Why the men were dragged through doors: because a Mennonite does not fight. A Mennonite cannot raise a hand in self-defense. Mennonites are called traitors, and so made to stand in front of the brigade, at the front of the line, human shields, the first to be hit. They were dragged through doors to prisons during the wars; their houses and barns were burned. The women stood outside the prisons and cried while the men were starved to death, were beaten.

Arline has sung the song in the Mennonite hymnal, the one

about the blessedness of those that are persecuted. She has looked at the pages of the *Martyr's Mirror*, maybe not all 1,140 pages of torture, of resolve, of imprisonment, of piousness, but some, some of the pages she has seen. She has read the accounts of the Anabaptists being stoned, being drowned, being pulled apart by oxen, being beheaded with axes, being stuck through with spears, being dragged by wild horses, being hung by ropes, being put into stocks, being buried alive, being burned alive. She has heard the story of the Snyders, who came on the boat of William Penn but left the land grant, left everything during the Revolutionary War to come to Ohio, to escape persecution. Always, for Arline, everything is lost. Arline walks around and around the house, her arms across her chest, pretending that everything is fine, is good, thinking thoughts of regret, of murder, of escape. The life of the party is at a party that is lasting a week. When he gets home what he wants is an ice pack, an aspirin, for someone to rub his shoulders. He could use something good to eat, a fresh start.

Arline will fill the bag with ice. She will screw on the top, bring a glass of water and two pills in her open palm.

Arline will not go back. She will go ahead and look just fine. The bad is not inside. It is outside. She will put an iron on the youngest child's arm to straighten her out. She will twist the arm of the one who can't talk. She will not give her food. The child cries and cries until her legs go bent, until her hair falls out, until she goes back under the bed and stops crying. Arline likes to hear her cry. She will take a broom and chase her out from under the bed. The sound of someone else crying is a good sound to Arline.

Arline is not looking at any child. Arline's eyes are out the window, ready to fasten onto a light in the driveway. Arline is ready with everything perfect. She is ready to talk to the life of the party about whatever he might want to talk about, the woman across the street, for instance, who is not as smart as Arline, who does not do anything right, who sees whatever she wants, who spends too much money, who wants her husband to work too hard.

Then the life of the party will fall on the bed and Arline will take off his shoes, his socks, his shirt. She will take off his pants, look through his pockets, look in all the flaps of his wallet. Then Arline will walk around and around the house. Arline cannot stop thinking. Arline walks and thinks about deeds, about faults, about amounts and things that are owed.

The life of the party gets to do whatever he wants, Arline thinks. Arline will never ask for help from anyone. Emerson and Robert live in the same town as she but she will not ask for help. She will never go back. She is not the weak in spirit. She is not the one in need. She is the one who is holding everything together, who is doing everything right. She is the one who has to make sure, who does without. She is not washing anyone's feet, wearing any prayer cap. Arline is living with the worldly and she is looking ahead and holding her head up high. Arline likes the word noble.

Arline will be the one who crosses her own ocean. She will be the one who finds the way to the Quaker college. She leaves the two children with the oldest one and she walks one, two, three, four miles, as far as it takes for her to have her own place in the row, to be the one who gets called on, to be the one with the right answer, with the most thought. Arline is not thinking about the life of the party anymore. She is not thinking about whether or not she is the best one for him. Now she is thinking about Sartre, about Kant, about Piaget, about the things that Paul said. Arline is not looking through wallets; she is looking up ahead, on past the horizon if there ever was one in this old steel town. She is looking past the strip mines, past the miles and miles of gray shale and fluorescent green pools and reflector orange pools of water. She is looking past the huge factories with the orange waterfall of molten steel, past the houses and houses of immigrants come to mind the orange waterfall twenty-four hours a day, past the green fields of the Mennonites, even past the black dirt of the Amish of Hartville. Arline is looking even further than Cleveland, even past the lake that is Erie, which is nothing at all but a clear sheet of ice for the wind to whip up its speed, to pick up bits of ice to make its presence better felt. Arline is not of this world, no sirree. Arline is having nothing of this dominant bitter world, no, not anymore.

What Arline needs now is an incident, a Remember-the-Maine of her existence and that is easy for someone like the life of the party. He decides the oldest child will not go out, will not be at any parties ever. He says no, Arline says yes, and then he pushes the oldest child down the steps to show Arline what's what and who's who. For Arline that is just what she was waiting for and she takes the three children in one day and moves them into an abandoned house while the life of the party is dancing the night away. And that is the end of that. That is the end of the life of the party in the life of Arline.

The life of the party is still the life of the party as far as I know.

At the abandoned house, Arline tears boards off windows, dusts, finds rhubarb, asparagus in the weeds. She brings home boxes of clothes, says to the children, "Go ahead, pick what you want." There are dances on Friday nights, a job for the days of the week, a Church of the Brethren for Sundays, the Quaker college for night classes.

The life of Arline is a hard one, not a life for anyone weak, anyone who feels a little bit woozy. The life of Arline is a life that no one should have, that no one should see. It is a life of bad this and bad that, of nothing but one bad thing and then another bad thing and Arline never asked one person for help ever. She would rather do without. She would rather everyone would do without. There is nothing in this world that Arline needs.

Arline gets down on her knees in the basement of the little brick church and she washes feet. I am beside her. After she finishes, I will be the one to wash the feet of Arline and I get down on my knees and lift her feet and place them in the white basin. I cup my hand and pour the water over the feet of Arline, over the corns, the blisters, the hard calluses on the feet of my mother, the feet that have walked a very hard, a very mean road.

My mother in one second gave me everything on earth. I can hit the fence posts from now until the sky turns red and it is all mine: dances on Saturday nights, gloves, streets, Portugal, Bahia, Oaxaca, France (I suppose, should I decide to go), my home here on the Lower East Side of New York City, my feet, these hands, a potato, that carrot, everything I could want, right here, right at this point, right now, and, at the end of this, even, a place to start.

Canton, Ohio

The shed is next to the house I am supposed to go to. It is the house where a woman sits with a handkerchief to her nose, where a grown-up sleeps with her knees up in the bed next to me, where a boy sleeps in the bed with me. We just came to this house from someplace I do not remember.

At night I sit on the floor behind the couch, mash soda crackers into a bowl, then lick them out with my tongue. The boy who sleeps in the bed with me puts his head on the floor against a wall, then pushes his legs up and wobbles there, hanging by his heels in the middle of the wallpaper. The grown-up bangs the screen door against the house, gets in a car. The chair where the woman sat opening and closing and folding and tearing a handkerchief is empty. I want to see my eggs, just to look.

There are three eggs. If I pick one up, my hand is sandy inside all day, a special hand.

Behind the house I am supposed to go to is an alley and children play there. They hold on to the edges of a blanket, then wave it up and down until someone jumps inside. They fold dolls into cloths, then lay them in cardboard boxes. The boy who sleeps in the bed with me chases boys who have sticks for guns, baseballs, bats.

At night, I see the eggs on the roof falling off.

The woman sitting in the chair with the handkerchief to her nose is not my mother.

The eggs are stuck inside a bowl of twigs and feathers and gum wrappers, and a finger of the roof curls up, brown, around it.

When the girls in the alley notice me, they coo over me, pat my head, the head that has no hair, then put their fingers on their braids.

The grown-up leads me out onto the back porch and puts me down between her legs on the step in front of her. She rubs oil on my head and tells me her secret.

The sky is white.

I climb the ladder, rest my stomach on the top rung and pet my eggs. I pick them up with two fingers, tuck them into my pocket, then inch down. I hold my dress up with the eggs in it, in the pocket, and skip to the house to show everybody inside. But someone pulls the pocket open, looks in, puts my arms in the air, pulls my dress off, throws it in the tub, turns on the water. The dress puffs up, blue in the water. I get the pieces of the shell on my finger, put them in my mouth, and swallow them all.

All Things Are Labor

All this happens under the moon.

The place where the boys come is our home. In twos or threes or all alone, they slow down on Fulton, glide without motors, steer without power, park without light.

Our home is below South Street. Inside are wood floors, plastered walls, porcelain sinks, ceilings, a toilet. Outside, candy stores, shortcuts.

Downtown is one door up.

We can make pizza from a box, lemonade from a can. The boys are happy to help.

The boys are the sons of machinists, the sons of iron workers, the sons of television-store owners, pawnbrokers, plumbers. They are Greg Muntz of Muntz Iron and Steel, Clark Kaufman of the Kaufman Jewelry Shop, Mick Finn of Finn's Scrap Metal.

Our fathers were dandies, our mothers say. Our fathers never worked one day. They had ten pairs of shoes, six suits; every hair was perfect. They were gallivanting, highfalutin', waltzing, rip-roaring, indiscreet.

They are off the subject.

Our dads. Our dads. Our dads. Our dads.

The boys want us to go for a ride. They want us to swim at their club, fly in their Cessnas. They want to press us up against a doorway, bend us over furniture, pull us up by the waist. Out on their lawn, beyond the rectangle of light from a kitchen window, the boys want us to get down on our knees. They want us to feel their jean zippers, their hearts on our chest. They want to roll us top and bottom until our hair is matted, our mascara messed and we are new-mown-grass-covered. Then they want us to go back inside to meet their dads.

We are hair sprayed, teased, ratted, curled, or ironed. Lined up across the hood of a car, leaning back on the windshield, we are all legs crossed left.

All arms and elbows and hips and feet.

Their dads in armchairs mention potato chips, soft drinks, tell the boys to be polite.

We are underneath. They come quiet as eels with their engines cut, their auxiliary on, their green lights red. They wait in their cars, checking the dashboard, their rearview mirrors, an upstairs light.

Our home smells of mittens on the radiator, boiling potatoes, clothes-dryer exhaust, the head of a newborn, a string mop.

Our mothers' shoes are on the sidewalk.

We do not like the boys to be polite.

We put the bottles on the floor by the refrigerator, wipe off the table, rinse the sink, take the garbage out. Our mothers are out snipping plastic goo, working a counter. Our brothers snapped into pajamas, our sisters flannelled in. We lift the slat of the Venetian blind, look for a car painted red, a car painted black.

Their dads ask if we are hungry, tell us to look at ourselves. We are so skinny. They want to know if we are cold, if those are goose bumps. They say that they themselves have gotten a little out of shape.

Who we are is the girls. As soon as the sun goes down we are out on the stoop, thinking about the future, our future.

Every boy is right. Each place is good. We are sneaking them upstairs, jumping over fences, dragging them through back doors, holding up fake IDs, saying go fast, faster.

Saying let's, let's, let's.

The road is empty.

What I said is not true, not a hundred percent. Not every boy is right; some boys are not right. To the not-right boys' faces we are polite. We tell them not tonight, maybe tomorrow night. We are exhausted tonight, we say, we cannot meet one more dad.

We will not remember our mother over a broken toilet, standing there ironing. We will remember her at night. She wraps her hair up high, turns a porch light on, twists her skirts through two doors, walks even past uptown, comes back.

Of the right boys, the boys that are not wrong, there are always more boys and better boys. Boys on strings. Boys on fingers. Knee boys. Under the thumb boys. Hand boys. Every night boys.

Our boys. Our boys. Our boys. Our boys.

Our homes are close enough to pass Cokes through windows, close enough to listen for a next-door kid. Close enough for one wardrobe, one set of makeup, one box of Kotex.

Our front door is oak. Our mother says our house is solid.

The rain hits the tops of leaves, the lids of trash cans, the tin of a porch roof, a shop awning. It is cool in the alley, warm in the street, cold on the corner. Under the streetlights the rain is snow. At midnight the sky is white, the street black, the doors closed. There is no moon to be under, no cars.

Some of this may be made up.

The boys say their dads ask what happened to us. Their dads say they want us to come back, the boys say, but not tonight. Tonight, their dads want them to work inventory. Tonight, their dads are making them drive to the club. Tonight their dads want to discuss Europe, prep school, whatever the boys might want, the boys say. Their dads have come down to earth, done a turnaround.

Our home is peeling. Our brother has croup. The faucet will not turn off. Our mothers save grocery receipts in a coffee can. Out there, our mothers say, pointing up above the building roofs, are tax collectors, rocks, dirt, the courts.

We rinse diapers in the toilet, scrub socks in the sink, shave in the tub, paint on peel-off eyeliner.

Our mothers say bad taste is one dot more than is needed, anything got and spent.

I cannot remember the end of this, only sitting up straight saying stop.

Our mothers wear prayer caps, unhook their garters, slip down on their knees to wash feet and so do we, but this is of the day and not the night. All things are labor, our mothers say. They do not ride the road at night, so fast. They do not see what is in the wind, like we do at night, on our nights.

Our nights. Our nights. Our nights. Our nights.

Traffic is bad.

It is an off night. The boy has big feet, whines and whines, then lies. But I am polite, ride in the car painted blue.

The moon is bright white.

In a cornfield: a blue car leaves a dirt road, bumps over a ditch, rides across the furrows. The corn is ocher and laid flat, so it is fall, late fall, since the white fuzz of frost hugs the blades of grass, the wormy roots of corn.

It is the end of night.

My child is the most beautiful thing in the world. She looks at me without seeing, turns toward touch, does not know where she is, grabs any object, curls up like a smile when the sun comes up, then cries and cries and cries till night.

Yellow Light

Ohio is the place that she came to me.

Late, digging her fingernails in, ready to have what is only fair, what is only right.

Not a word at first. Nothing but the yellow light.

Me, I was dark in the heart. Eyes can't see. Ears don't hear. Mouth won't talk, just dark, dark, dark. The rusted belt steel trap jaws clamped tight. I was thinking, thinking, thinking, how to get out, how to get out of Ohio. A few first periods, then held down in a convertible Impala. Then, there I was, washed up, unwed. I waved my arms. "Here, here, over here," I said, "Pick me. I'm pregnant."

She did.

Her and that yellow light.

Trusting, trusting a teenager to feed and burp and not drop.

It was not easy for her, for the yellow light. My bones too small, no dilation, the doctor coming in to start again the forcedness, saying, "You had fun getting this way," but it was not true, was not. Then, finally, another doctor, coming in, wheeling me away, saying, "This is my patient now."

Then, there she was. Surrounded by light, by yellow light.

Inside, diapers to fold, apricot sauce to spoon off the chin, vitamin drops to remember to give.

Outside, all manner of beings: the rapacious, the vicious, the beaten-down, the repressed, the ones who try to live without dreams, who try to settle for.

At night they rise up. Pajama tops flipped up to show where something vital got cut out. "Lookey. Lookey," they say. Here a stump of arm, there a metal plate. A finger lost on the press, in the cutter. "Top that. Top that," they say. The scar across the neck. Fingers held up to say this close, this close to it.

All deserted by parents. All beaten. Each an unfavorite child. All babies murdered in their cribs.

We came here to die is what they do not say.

In the meantime they give something to fight against, something not to pick.

There must be another place, an outside of this quicksand of Ohio.

Inside she screams, lifts her tummy in the air, then kicks, kicks, kicks. Other times it is hands on the mouf, mouf, moufy. Ha-ha. he-he, ha-ha. Eyes held tight shut, wide open, tight shut. Like a child, like a regular child.

Those dimples on a pointed finger.

The overalls unsnapped, corduroy, red.

The Keds.

Pick up. Pick up. Pick up. Hold me.

Over and over.

An adolescent and her kid.

Me and her.

Stuck in the ooze of Ohio, this field of malcontents. First four years at the factory, the baby at the stone church day care. Make a rubber glove. Dip a rubber glove. Strip a rubber glove. Powder a rubber glove. Inspect a rubber glove. Box and bag a rubber glove. Vats of white latex. Rows of fluorescent lights. Ceramic hands. Put on a hairnet and shut up about the coagulant and how it eats eyes, shut up about the effluent in the creek, the talc clogging the lung, the FDA, the strike. Shut up and show an incision, talk about a broken leg.

Belong, belong to this Ohio.

Downtown is deserted. No more fancy shops. No more shops at all. No more of the theater with the castle top, the aquamarine ceiling. No more of teenage fun. No more factories, no more stores, no more new immigrants every year, no more strikes, no more government cheese. Even the train won't come to Canton anymore.

She came from another place with that yellow light. She came to me. Now I have to have a place that is warm. I have to have money left over to buy food, money for one thing and then another. I cannot have even one sick day. I cannot have one more bad thing happen that costs money.

The doctor, the one that saved me, says, "No one will ever do this to you again," and gives me what he calls protection. He takes me in his office, gives me a lecture about Eros, other words I am too ashamed to admit I do not understand.

Then, finally, it happens, a miracle. Just a chance meeting. A forklift operator from the factory takes me to his neighbor's house, a plumber's house. We sit in the plumber's den with his four children, all grown, about my age. We sit and look at slides of Boston University, where one of the girls goes to college. I see brick and ivy, a dorm room, a building she calls the student union, the library. Then we see slides from another college. Temple University. The other daughter is studying art. She is there in the art studio, her hair up in a bun, in painter's pants and a big sweater. She is smiling at us, a painting behind her. Every slide is something I could look at for an hour, but I am afraid to say anything. I am seeing all I can see. Then they show slides of a trip to the Bahamas. I did not know a place like this could be in the world, all blue and full of white boats. We are eating ice cream. They are all laughing about one thing or another. This is a family, I think. Then it is time to go out on the driveway and look through the son's telescope, to look at the Seven Sisters, the rings around Saturn, the face of the moon.

I have seen. Now that I have seen, I cannot go back.

I hide the implements of escape. I am going. I am going. I am going. I snap her into her overalls. Hang on, hang on, I say, and pack up a knapsack, sling it across my back. We are off, my flat feet light across the muck, at first afraid, then it is headfirst through the field, the leaves of corn, slap, slap, slap, slapping. I am dodging obstacles. The boys grab but don't catch. I am safe and infertile with my IUD, and, following her, the light I find in front, I sneak across the border and out.

Welfare

There is nothing but what is here. What is here is the thin-boned child left for dead but she is not dead. She is something, my thin-boned child. My child. She is alive with cracked lips, crusty eyes. Inside her mouth is a dark color; there is something wrong with her tongue. I cannot look.

We have been forced here, backed up to here, then left. I cannot take my eyes off of my thin-boned child, even if I wanted to, which I never, ever want to do.

Look, you can see her now. She is there by the side of the road, waiting for anything moving, anything that is out of place. If something squeals, is run over, dragged, she is on it, holding it up high, bringing it back, trying to keep it from biting, trying to keep it from coming completely apart.

Me, I have not caught one whole animal, not even a lizard, a bug. Everything I find is already picked apart, already dead. What I want is to find something for the thin-boned child, something to bring to the thin-boned child, something to make it better, something for her that she needs but by the time I get there it is just intestines with fur on it, a head with maggots, a few bones already cleaned white or just the empty highway. I am the one who is supposed to get the animals, supposed to provide, but I have not caught one. I look for a can, a bag with the taste of salt still on it. I dig for water, like this.

The mountains do not get closer, no matter how much I walk.

I did not teach the thin-boned child to talk. It is not just the tongue.

She sucks on a flattened horned toad, holds it in her teeth and makes that black goo smile. She takes the stingers out of scorpions, puts them in her mouth, lets them whip. She knocks a lizard on a rock, clamps it on her ear. She collects thorns.

I cannot take my eyes off the thin-boned child. I love to see the thin-boned child. I love the thin-boned child. You would, too, if you saw her moving there between the saguaro, hiding behind an organ pipe, a sagebrush, her hair matted and wild.

What she does with the animals: she keeps them alive. She has a stick to keep the animals from dragging themselves away. She doesn't let the buzzard get anywhere close. She feeds them flies and prickly pear. Then she breaks off a part of the animal and puts it right in her mouth with the horned toad. It could be the foot of a rabbit, the tiny leg and tail of a mouse, or a wing with feathers.

That thin-boned child is something to see.

There is more here than you would think. I have my claw, my beak, my shredded tire. At night there are howls, the snorts of javelinas, hoots and wills. Once a deep buzz of bees went by and made it dark night at day. I dig a hole for the worst of the heat. I put stones in my skirt for cool. At night they are warm.

There is no one looking for us, no one looking out for us. We are left for dead but we are not dead. The cars with the thick-boned people go back and forth and forth and back. They seem to look but they see nothing. Their windows are rolled up or blacked out, their air conditioners are on, their eyes are glazed.

What we are looking for is something small that we can use. That is all we need, a little bit, something that happened by chance, something common like a broken piece of glass, some string, a book of matches: just a small thing where there is nothing but what is here to find.

There were boys that went through here on horses, then went south. There are the cars, like I said, but the cars are nothing. The boys were something. They had leather straps, bags and canteens, buckles and flaps. They said there was nothing from here to where they started out from but empty this and empty that. They said they had seen enough of thin-boned girls and their thin-boned children; they were sorry, but they could not stop, they could not talk. Then they came back and they gave the thin-boned child a knife.

It is the thin-boned child that always gets something.

She makes noises. When those boys gave her that knife, she ran after them, jumped up, grabbed onto a cuff, held on, made her gurgles, her deep nargles, her harguts, her grunts, her grooves. They kicked her off.

"You ought to teach that thing to talk," they said, "Just in case."

I should. I should teach her to say thank you, please, and can I, but I can't. Whoever taught me to talk was all wrong. Not one word turned out to be true, turned out to be right. They went around and around making more and more of themselves and nothing of me. They all ended up saying no, saying can't, saying don't.

The thin-boned child can, though; the thin-boned child does. She makes a bat with cactus thorns, stone-sharpened pieces of bumper with coyote bone handles, a fan belt with a rock on the end, traps, and slicing things. She made a lookout. At night she has a fire, a bird in a hubcap pot, soup in turtle-shell bowls. She took the cactus that looks like a dead cactus skeleton and made a house. She took rocks and made a floor. She brought back a piece of blue plastic from the road and made a roof with a gutter that empties into a barrel. There she is, crawling into her barrel at the hot part of the day. See, she is splashing now, hitting the water with her horned toad.

Me, I am in my hole.

For me, there is more than what is here. Things I do not want to teach the thin-boned child.

A redheaded buzzard sits there on her pole, waiting for something cast-off. Coyotes close in at night. Everyday the thin-boned child goes further and further and further out. Each day she brings back more. She has a big-eared rabbit; blue hummingbird morsels; the head of a wolf; even, I swear, a goat. She can use a bottle cap, a cigarette filter, an old snakeskin, a piece of barbed wire. The thin-boned child knows how to act. For the thin-boned child there is nothing but what is here and she is making something of it.

The day the bees came through she was down from her lookout and off behind them. That black goo is part honey, that's what I think.

She is making something of every little thing. One of the cars with the thick-boned people skidded off the road and rolled over and over, then stopped. The thin-boned child was on it, dragging out the thick-boned people and bringing them back, squealing and not all of one piece. There were parts not appendaged, dangling, snakes of insides dropping, drippings. She is keeping them alive with the rest of her animals, using yucca to wrap the places that are falling out, using the aloe vera plant to stuff up holes, making them eat the root of osha, the branches of the ephedra. At night she makes her soft noises, coos at them, brushes back their hair, offers the stinger-less scorpion, the buzzard foot. At first they did not move. Now they sit up by her fire, make noises back, clap when she makes those thin-boned child faces. They even sing. She has them weaving juniper to make a bed, pulling feathers for their pillow. I don't know if she is breaking off pieces of them, if that was a finger I saw in her mouth with the horned toad and the honey. I am afraid to look.

She does not say a word about it. I already told you she doesn't talk.

One day she took down the blue plastic roof and put the thick-boned people on it along with all her things. She put my claw, my beak, my shredded tire on top and started off. What she came to was the rolled-over car. The thin-boned child pulled on this, pushed in that. She put the thick-boned people in the back, her things in the trunk. She got in, started it up, and drove it right back onto the road.

One thing I know. It is wrong to teach a poor child no; it is wrong to teach a poor child can't, or don't.

We are on the road now, me and the thin-boned child and the thick-boned people. I think we are taking them home. They look out from under their blue plastic blanket and smile. We were left for dead but we are not dead. The thin-boned child is turning the lights on. She is taking the horned toad out of her mouth, putting it on her knee, opening her plastic bottle full of goat blood or wolf blood or rat blood, taking a sip and passing it around. The thick-boned people lean over the seat. They gurgle. They charl. They grunt. The thin-boned child has taught us how to talk, they say. I make a nargle. They nod, touch me on the shoulder. What we are is gathered together. There is the deep down sound of the engine, of things finally moving. What we have with us is the bat with spikes, the sharpened pieces of muffler, the rabbit feet with their deep claws, the hubcap knife blades, a lighter that works.

The thin-boned child knows how to act.
She is on the road with the windows rolled down, making those noises, spitting out that black goo, heading into the city with everything that she dragged off the road, took apart and put back together, and is now offering up.

Arkansas

They disco in my millet field. Down there among my ticks and chiggers, my toads, my new crop of blue-tailed lizards, they flash between the stalks. He, in his shirt of photographs, she, in her white dress, which billows, then twists around her legs like silk or rayon, but it is something better. It leaves trails. I can see them from here. The crickets sing about dimming on the lights tonight to the moon, but it is full, ochre on the millet.

They slide hip to hip on the lightning-bug dance floor. Pass butyl nitrate between them, then toss it down. Tomorrow I will find the brown bottle.

It is my proof.

The millet, now over my head, started smaller than a mustard seed. I threw it in arcs, keeping parallel to the fence. I did not miss a spot. With a tractor, I will turn under the millet and plant fescue seed, scattering it on the clods of overturned dirt. Then I will bend on my knees, dragging a burlap bag behind me, and sprig Bermuda, pinching the starts into my land, my earth that wants to slide down the hill to the creek, and that will, despite bags of 10-20-10 I will pour onto the seed, despite the PVC pipe I will suck on to draw water from the pond during the drought, despite every dime I have, because I cannot fight gravity, though I don't know it yet.

I pull the string on the lightbulb and crouch down under the window. They are there again. Lying on the rock by the pond. He leans on his elbow, pulls back his hair, which falls, wet, into his eyes. She rests her head on her arms, smiles up at night. She points at a shooting star, but it would be too late, even if he looked, which he doesn't. His fingers touch, or barely touch (I cannot tell from here) the line from her leg to her rib. She rolls into him and he is ready, his hand circling the skinny part of her back. I flatten my hand and put it here, at the same place, on my back. The pond is a mirror; the light on it lines to do. He opens his wallet, pulls out money, which he rolls tight. They put it to their nostrils, leave it, then rise to something that sounds like ringing, ringing, ringing a bell. Tomorrow I will search the willows, but the red-winged blackbird has already beaked the hundred-dollar bill into her nest and I am afraid of the father, who swoops.

I worry over my field. Downhill from the pond a patch of red clay and shale grows larger and the furrows deepen. They are slicing their way through the pond bank to break it so the water will rush out on them and they will be riverbeds, if only for the seconds it will take to empty my pond. I lift out the clumps of clay with a posthole digger, then shovel the holes large. I fill white buckets with loam from the woods, mix in manure, then pour this into the holes. In the middle of each I plant a pine seedling. They will have time, their roots zooming through this soil, to love the idea of being pines, with the wind in their needles, so even steel will not stop their roots by the time they hit the clay.

It is still. The moment before dusk. The myrtle recedes: the phlox advances. I walk my land, watching my purple flowers turn to black lights, my mimosa close its leaves, my pines rise up, separate themselves. The ground drops from under me when the silence hits, then rushes back with the crickets and they are there, but closer. She stands on the fence, holds on to a tree and revolves her hips. He is below, both arms resting on the fence, smoking. I follow their eyes to the field and it is full. Bare-chested men circle their hips with their hands above them, then they back bend on one arm. Women flow by, then whirlpool, their heads staying put, or maybe snapping around too quick to see. They all know the same step, and I mimic them, first getting the feet, then the body, then the arms. A truck comes over the hill, its lights pointing up first, then down on me. I sidestep to the garden, bend over the squash, then raise up and wave when they pass. I watch the red lights go down the road, turn and cross the bridge, then head up the hill, gears straining. I look back at the fence, but it is empty. The millet, its leaves now crisp, rustles in the wind.

The runoff from the pond flows into a ravine. Clumps of my field fall into it, then wash down the ditch along the road. If this is a wet fall and the ravine retreats to the pond, I will lose it. Already the cedar posts of the fence dangle, held by the barbed wire only. It is an omen. In the drought of August, I carry rocks to the edge, throw them in, then climb down, stack the stones against the sides. I mix cement, sand, and water; push it between the rocks.

Tomorrow, if it does not rain, the hired tractor will come to turn under the millet, putting the nitrogen back into the soil, putting back the matter that is organic. I walk the field with a crowbar, clearing rocks that might snag the blade. It is my part of the bargain and I work past sunset. I hoist a rock onto logs and roll it, grabbing the log it had rolled over and placing it before the rolling stone. It starts to drizzle, and I give up. Then, they are there, surrounding me in the middle of my millet field. From under the ground I hear someone sing about doing what you want to do, but to keep dancing and then I am, passed from partner to partner, pulled catty-corner to the music, until it is just me and the man in the shirt covered with the photographs, who holds both my hands and says, "We are leaving. You must come with us. This is only one place," and the crickets sing about not stopping, not stopping, don't stop, but I do, pulled back into my millet field.

I turn the millet under, plant the fescue and Bermuda, but before it can catch, it pours. The rain takes first the seed, then the sprigs, then the top soil and the millet underneath. The field gives into the ravine, then, when the pond goes, it all goes down into the creek, then to the Mulberry, to the Arkansas River, to the Mississippi, maybe even to the Gulf.

In the house, four rooms also sliding down the hill, though slower, I practice the dance steps, watching my reflection in the windows. I have perfected them, added flourishes. I put oil in the pot on the wood stove, pour in millet seed. When it browns, I add boiling water. It is the way to cook millet, I was told, by someone in my past; someone who is down the hill, past the Mulberry, past the Arkansas River, even further away than the Mississippi, across the Continental Divide, on the Colorado; someone I left to come to this farm, to this life, someone with whom I may have made something that would last if only I could speak the words of want, the words of desire, but instead I choose this, my own landscape, my own want, my own way, my own fault.

I Had a Farm in Arkansas

I wanted to write about my farm in Arkansas. "I raised millet, fescue, Bermuda, blue-tailed lizards, yarrow, daffodils, chiggers, one bluetick hound, mimosa, wild rose, pear, shag bark hickory, cattails, whippoorwills, one six-year-girl child, asparagus, paw-paw, toads, red winged blackbirds, and millions times millions of frogs." That's as far as I got. I wanted to write about how I had a frog farm. I was thinking about how my computer sounds like crickets, the cicadas, the night sounds on my farm. Then I heard three shots. Loud.

I live in Alphabet City, on the worst drug block in New York City.

I looked out my back window at the projects. I got a railroad, which is like a shotgun house in the south, so I got windows out the front and back of the building both. It's about 1:30 am. I see nothing.

I slip back to thinking about what it was like in Arkansas when the marsh out the back of my house would be full of the deafening sound of frogs fertilizing eggs. The way my bluetick hound would chase a rabbit to me when we would set out after midnight on a full moon night walk. The bright light and dark shadows. The dry leaves underfoot. The sound of owls. Then I hear sirens out the front. My front room flashes red light through the miniblinds, through the grate of my window gates.

Something bad's been in the air.

Things have been getting worse. There's a shakedown going on. What they call a sweep. The cops busted the pot dealers in the storefront. Word was they quit making their payments to the cops. Next we got coke down there. I'm talking like the next day. We've always had the teenagers on each end of the block. They're not holding, but stash it somewhere down the block. In a trash can, under a car, in a crevice in a building. They get busted; they're juveniles. Tonight, I came home about six. There's no teenagers anywhere and the sidewalks are full of very nervous drug buyers, looking up and down the street, asking each other, shrugging their shoulders. I've been here ten years. I pay attention always, but I try not to look like it.

I go to the front window. I hear the kid yelling, a group of kids over him. He's still alive, I think. Probably shot in the legs. That's the way they do it. The cop cars are there; cops running up and down the street.

I go back to the blue light of my computer. I try to remember how the clear frog eggs with black specks grew into tadpoles and how the marsh started to dry up, and how I scooped the tadpoles up in buckets and carried them down the hill and across my pasture to the pond, hoping my neighbors wouldn't see me do it, or worse yet ask me, the urban Yankee outsider, what I was doing. Then I would let the tadpoles go into the brown water of the pond.

Here's what I think is happening. The cops are demanding more and more payoff from the dealers. So, the ones who get "cleaned up" are the ones that aren't paid up, or who aren't paying the higher amount. This is the story. Some guy across the street called the cops and took over pictures of the dealers. Next thing you know, he's been beat up, bad, by the dealers. It's happened more than once.

I hear more sirens. The ambulance is here and they're taking their good old time getting the bed out of the back.

It was my daughter who saw it first. How the pond boiled in tadpoles. We loved to watch their feet emerge, their tails disappear. We would float in inner tubes in the pond during the hot part of the day. Soon, the frogs would hang in the water, their hands, arms, and legs dangling, looking at us with their big yellow eyes, just enjoying, too, an Arkansas afternoon.

Now the cops are shining their flashlights back and forth on the sidewalk, looking for evidence. They look so out of place down here, the plainclothes cops. Their big muscles, their stockiness, their healthy skin, their postures, their mustaches. No one in New York City wears mustaches except the leather guys and cops. Soon they are back in their cars and gone. The street is back to its scary night self.

"I had a farm in Arkansas," I start again to write. I write of the sound of a lightning crack so loud I thought it hit my little house. The next day, walking my field, I saw the burn mark spiraling down my pine like someone had stuck in a knife and going round and round had split the bark. I think of the sound of rain on my tin roof, the sound of the logs settling in the wood stove, falling down into the orange coals. I think of the sound of the chains as I lifted them out of the back of my car and laid them in front of my tires, drove over them, plopped down on the ice and fastened them and the sound of the chains clapping on the ice as I headed up the hill home.

Then I hear it, coming from my back window, beyond the schoolyard, from the courtyard of the projects, the sound of dogs fighting. The growls, the squeals, the barking, and more squeals that seem to go on and on, then silence.

I go back to the writing, trying to decide if I am going to tell the story of when the sheriff shot my dog to warn me, when the sound of the dogs start up again. The growls, barking, squeals, the squealing, squealing, squealing.

I planted a garden in my backyard here. My little piece of Arkansas, I say. The lot next to me has chickens with big talons, roosters, corn, roses, cars. My little piece of Puerto Rico, says Angel, who broke the city lock and put on his own. I got iris, foxglove, pine, sage, morning glories, bees, forsythia, dogwood, peppermint, butterflies, comfrey, gladioli, four o'clocks, bluegrass, fern, and even, I don't know where it came from, a big old poke salad plant. There's several hundred families in the apartment building and the projects that look down on this little garden, see me working. I wish they could hear what I've heard, those nights I would watch the clouds pass over the face of the moon, hear the whizz of wind in the pines, the sound of the cicadas, the crickets, the whippoorwills, the owls, and my frogs down at the pond croaking thank you, thank you, thank you all night long.

On Poetics:
Ma Ripple's Last Words

Ma Ripple and her ant farms.

She's over there now on Eleventh Street with her nose to the glass, her eyes to the tunnels, making a spectacle.

"More helpful creatures never existed," she says.

"If you were to be in trouble, say you were stranded at the side of the road, and you needed help, pretty soon another ant'd come to the rescue.

"Ants act just like every minute was an opportunity to do good," Ma Ripple says.

She's got ten farms, propped up around her on top of cardboard boxes. She could turn a complete circle and, if she ignored the space between, it'd be ant farms and nothing but ant farms to the end of her world.

Ma Ripple says the world is closing in on her. She says she's got to learn fast. She will have to decide. She's got ten more days on her two years left to live. Her time is short to be on this earth, to be in her New York, on this Eleventh Street, to sit on her stoop, to make a Ma Ripple impact. She says she's getting down to bare bones, she's cut the fat, she's a skinflint that's gone back to the farm. Back to the canals, the veins in the sand, back to the arteries. Right back to nature.

The kids pick up their skateboards, come over and stick their eyes in the space between where the ant farms connect. They are looking at Ma Ripple.

Ma Ripple says, "Get out of my sight." She is not nodding politely to anyone anymore, she says. She is not going to service any more small talk. She is not going to be seduced by a swaying hip, a shy eye, no matter how charming, no matter how cute. Not one more human being is going to get her off her track.

The kids act as if Ma Ripple is a TV they can sit in front of. They want to learn about nature. They want to see an ant farm. They want to be doctors, biologists, entomologists. Come to Eleventh Street between B and C and ask them; they'll tell you.

They circle the ant farms on the outside. "Look," they say, and point to an ant carrying a piece of ant, a grain of sand.

"So watch already," Ma Ripple says. "You look you see them touching their antlers. Do you think they're talking about a mean boss? A nasty husband? A snitty sister? No way. Their little lives are short. They are not smelling out a lucky break, feeling for a sap."

Ma Ripple decides to study the particular. She wants a one-on-one experience with an ant. She wants to know another individual intimately who is also going to die before winter. So Ma Ripple picks one ant, names it Gertrude and, with her finger to the glass, follows Gertrude's little life. "Gertrude is not a chump," Ma Ripple says. "Gertrude does not hesitate. Look how fast she meets another ant, then goes on about what she is about. Is Gertrude sitting around complaining about having such skinny legs? Is Gertrude's mind on how easy she could break in two at the waist? About how anytime there's anything good, it's spread out across the kitchen floor?"

Ma Ripple sees Gertrude slant up a canal, then help a friend drag a boulder to the top of a hill. Gertrude pushes from behind. She pulls from ahead. Gertrude makes it to the top, to the little fake barn and little fake trees and the little fake shed.

"Yo, Ma Ripple," a kid says, "Are these real? Are these real ants?"

Ma Ripple squints up from the ant farms. She looks up at the kids, the buildings, then up at the rectangle of sky above Eleventh Street, then back down to her ant farms, to what she sent away for and assembled herself, to what she has just right.

"Check it out," a kid says. "Check it out."

"One little ant and another little ant and another . . ." Ma Ripple starts to say, but Ma Ripple's eyes are beginning to daze over with ants, the whole circle of them. Ma Ripple and her ant farms: the constant avalanches, the up and down, and back and forth, the on and on of it. Joy, tragedy, etc.

"Now I lost Gertrude," Ma Ripple says.

Ma Ripple is not thinking about her own little life. About the phone ringing help. The do this and do that, the gimme, gimme, gimme or the much obliged. She is not thinking about the poor little about-to-be-made-an-orphan Ripple. No, right now, Ma Ripple is in the middle of one continuous line of ant.

"I can't stand it," Ma Ripple says, "The beauty of it. The sheer, by that I mean the complete and overwhelming beauty of it, and here I am, surrounded."

"Cool," a kid says, "Ma Ripple is completely cool."

"The ants and the ants and the ants," Ma Ripple says. "The ants do not come easy. The first one, the little queen ant, delivered 'Live Shipment,' delivered 'Fragile,' delivered 'Rush.' Delivered to me to be put in a closet, to incubate, to make the itty-bitty baby ants, to make the ant-nation, the spectacle; each little ant, one little part, following the next little ant, making up a whole ant-story, heading towards who-knows-where, towards who-knows-what little ant-end?"

"Shit, I can't see," a kid says, "Can I get in there? Can I get in the middle, too?"

"Hurry up." Ma Ripple says, "you got to act fast. Your time is short. You will have to decide. You look. You'll see all that. You'll see how you can do, but it may not be as easy as you thought, as easy as you hoped, as easy as it seemed outside."

X

X rips sheets in twos, then threes, then fours. He files away bars, digs under walls, lands on his feet.

"Leavenworth," he says.

We are at Odessa. We have been to Mars, to Lynch's, to Rivington, to Five Roses, to Billy's. Now we are having breakfast. He is telling me where he's been.

"Coney Island," he says. "My truck." X points in the direction of Tompkins Square Park, then full of the blue plastic homes of the homeless, open all night.

Everything is held together by coat hangers, frayed yellow rope and black and silver tape.

"You got your inside and you got your outside," X says. We are sitting in the truck. He is fiddling with wires. "On the outside, if you can make it go, anything goes, goes on forever." The truck bounces on. Stops. X pushes in this, pulls out that. "On the inside anything goes, too, but not forever. You got time to consider inside."

47

This part concerns getting there. X is looking at the gray road, the gray river, the gray bridge. He is looking for the green light. He is dialing the radio knob. He is swerving away from bumps and jarring things. He is trying for the smooth ride, the right speed.

Out there, the driftwood, sand, a tire, a blue plastic bottle, the smell of sewage, huge yellow condoms, suds.

It is my job to walk in the front door. X says, "Let the muscles of your face fall to the ground. Put 'Telstar' on in your head, or 'Wipe Out.' Pretend there's a hole in the top of your skull that you breathe through and your body is a lung. No, pretend you are molecules, or better yet just atoms. Pretend it is next year and it is all over. "Anything," X says, "but this."

I see X running; his feet are wheels. He heads toward a line in the middle of the screen. Railroad signs and cactus fly by, but the world is round and there is no end.

I am wearing a pink suit with big buttons, pink shoes, a pink hat, and a pink purse. I look as if I belong here. Like a dancer that married well or someone widowed early. I should have a small dog on a leash, but I cannot think of everything.

When I come out, X is on the street, "What happened?" I say.

"Nothing," X says.

"I thought you had it worked out," I say.

"Me too," says X. I decide I am never going above Fourteenth Street again. No matter what.

Four days and no X.

"Booking," X says. He has a gash on his forehead, a slice down his arm, a broken lip. "Pissing on the street," X says.

X's voice. I forgot to tell you about X's voice, his curling-up voice, his fingering voice, his nodding-out voice. It is a voice perfect for a big chest, a heavy beard. It is a voice that blows out walls, gets one over, comes on over the telephone.

X grabs the bartender, holds him against the wall, pushes him down on the pool table, releases him. I see the guy run behind the bar, crouched down on the phone.

"We better get out of here," I say. I am holding coats, watching the door. Outside X tells me he studied under Harold Bloom. "Are you sure it wasn't the other Bloom?" I ask. We watch the cops, billy clubs up, run into the bar, then we cut west on Thirteenth.

"Harold Bloom," X says. "It was Harold Bloom."

Day-Glo trails of light through the water in Guatemala. A blue room. I am the one that took you to Palenque, X, do you remember? Me, the Mennonite in black, on a topless beach in Mexico, looking for X.

"And here he is," I say, "Here he is, right here." A needle in a haystack, my X.

The radio plays only for X, only for X and me.

X is riding in a cab. The white light on the blue water. The Verrazano Bridge. A tulip. The Manhattan there are no words about. "When you are in love, the whole world looks different," X says.
"Ahh," the driver says, "Everything is as though so real."

X is gone again. Booking. This time a sweep of peddlers. "Plainclothes," he says, "Very plain."
X gets a flat-brimmed Amish hat. "Do you like me," X says, "now that I can do the dance?"

My great-great-great-etc. stood outside the prisons in Bern, hands two by two, palms up. "Take me, take me," he said, she said, and they did, but still there were more: more for the prisons, the fenced-in places, the holes of ships, bowled cells run over with them: the Anabaptists, the Amish, the Mennonites, the Brethren. Latched below, they lay down beside the water, passed from one world to another, from prison to prison. To us there is no outside.

X is living in the park. He is sleeping on Junior's bench. He is warming his hands on Junior's wood. He is asking Steve for five dollars. He is moving into the squat on Thirteenth. He is getting stabbed in the back with scissors. He is wearing welcomes. He is buying, cooking, smoking, buying, cooking, smoking, buying, cooking, smoking, buying, cooking, smoking, buying, cooking, smoking, etc.
No hat, no heat, no water, no shoes.
"Oh, X," I say, looking down. "Oh, X, you are mismatched."

Me, I am in Bellevue. Something genetic, recessive. The woman next to me says, "You concentrate on here." She points to the middle of her forehead, "And you get down, think about what you want, a boyfriend back, for example, a new outfit, or the end of this. It will happen, believe me," she says, "and fast. It will all be over before you know it."

I choose the boyfriend back. X was a boyfriend, or something like a boyfriend.

The old Electric Circus. On New Year's Eve, I see X wait in line for his hug, hold hands in a circle, talk about coming back, keeping coming back. "Hello my name is Richard. I am an addict," X says with that voice, that X voice, from that X chest, from X.

"Hello, Richard." the room says.

This is not the real ending.

We are tying up quilts, sitting on the Samsonite, checking the tailpipe. The rope reaches twice over, the top is down, the inside out. I cross my feet on the dashboard, fix my head forever in the crook of X's neck.

"Thataway," I say, pointing to the windshield. X turns the key, and just like that, he makes it go, go on and on.

M

M is beside himself. I am outside. His door will not close, he says. It is off its hinges. The more he closes, the more it opens. He says it does not make sense.

The door is the door to his store, which is not a store but a used-to-be-store-space that is piled this high with broken lamps, boxes of magazines, socks that don't match, paintings, and amps.

M is filled up. He is overflowing. He is running down the street, waving to the men in the Hawaiian clothes. He is giving the man with the broken eye a dollar. He is feeling his back pocket, touching his lips, smoothing his hair, pulling down his hat. He is feet first, everywhere leaving parts of himself.

I have some of him here with me now. A doll made out of felt circles that hangs by its neck in my bathroom, a photo of a barbecue, a horse with two heads.

M says this is his lucky day. Always, he says, a twenty-second is a day for him for luck. We are walking to the place where I live. He is turning in circles. He is finding everything funny: the moon, for instance, the street. Everywhere is with the right side left upside down, the inside emptied out, the outside piled up in the middle. There are things that are swerving backward that cannot see where they are going, things with looks on their faces that are way too gleeful. We are bending over the railing, looking past the first thing, toward something that he must tilt my head to see.

Next we are coming down from seeing Morphine. We are riding in a cab. He is taking my legs and draping them over his legs. He is putting one hand then another on top of mine. He is holding the felt doll up to the window for air. He is asking me if I want out, but I do not want out.

M. Look at m. Two round mounds of m and a straight-up part. M that makes so many things begin like musky, meadow, or melting or man. Oh, would that I could squeeze and squeeze and be with the M of m, hearing M, Mmmmmmm. M, this 3 that has fallen on its side.

M is giggling. He is turning in circles. He is trying to catch up to his feet, there ahead of him, way out in front.

Me, I am smiling to see the happy feet of M.

M is in a hurry. He does not have much time. He has to make money. He has to be careful or he will lose something. It is true. When he leaves, where he dropped his pants, are tokens and roaches, nickels and dimes.

M is the son of a father. He is looking for openings. He is scanning the crowd. He is changing the subject. He is moving fast. He says he got the once-over twice. He is smiling. He is touching the hair on everyone's arm. He is telling everyone to wait, to hold this, just a minute, he will be right back. Around the store are more and more people: the boys in the band, the jester, the merchant marine, Curtis, the child who wants a father, the mother with no husband, the young girl learning the guitar. He is walking across the street, turning in circles. He is slapping people on the back. He is touching his hat. He is having to be happy, to be the one in charge, the one with nothing wrong.

There are things I wish M could see: a spot on a dog that makes a perfect Florida, a rodeo in Huntsville, Arkansas, the light in Tupelo, Bisbee, Huehuetenango. The way he moves back and forth and forth and back.

There are things he should not tell: where he lives, who he lives with, how his father made his living, how his mother wrapped sandwiches, smoothed the tablecloth, how he loved the curve of her back, her long waist.

I have seen patterns that float and movement behind that. It is not just mice that catch the corner of my eye in this place on Eleventh Street between B and C. It is not bad luck that I came upon M, not completely.

M is not a grandfather, or a father, a sitter of babies, a collector, or buyer, or a counter of pennies. He is a maker of blue, a rider of cycles, a flyer of apart, a seer of empty. He is the man with a door that will not close, with the hole that will not be stopped up.

Webfoot

Something wasn't right from the beginning. With my lover. He had webbed feet, for example, but I'm told that is not that unusual. The real problem was this: he was just too beautiful. Someone can be too beautiful. It put me on edge. I was suspicious.

I had a rent-controlled apartment and he moved in right away.

Next thing I know he'll change the locks, and my stuff will be on the street, I thought.

But no. He was perfect. Always had the rent. He paid his way. Something was wrong.

He never ate. He never drank. He never pissed. He never came. His skin was beautiful, but poreless.

"You're not human," I said to him one night and he said, yes, I was right. He wasn't human. He spilled the beans. He said he was from some planet; I forgot the name; he told me the galaxy, but, like, I don't even know where the boroughs are so I didn't catch the exact location.

"We have a housing problem," he said. "I was sent to get the scoop on housing here: rent control, zoning, rent stabilization, landlord/tenant regulations . . .

I said that was okay, that I was an immigrant, too.

"We're all citizens of the universe," I told him. I soothed him. I held his hand. I massaged his webbed feet. I rubbed his poreless brow. I cuddled him like a child.

Then I explained how the building had gone co-op; that I had to be out in ten days and had nowhere to go.

"Try Jersey City," he said, and disappeared.

Our Landlord

My landlord has taken over the world. He is collecting all the rent. He is out in the hall. He has a key to your lock.

He says you got your kitchen, your half-bedroom, your bathroom, so it adds up to three, to a three bedroom, check the records, if you want.

There is a new world order: my landlord. He is renovating China; he is sorry, but they will have to move out until he is finished. Russia, he says, is not listed as stabilized. France was not ever rent-controlled. Poland will get the keys when it pays the deposit. He went to Brazil and installed new appliances he found on the street, like stoves with gas leaks and refrigerators without doors, then he raised their rent. This he does all over the world: first, second, third, it's all the same now. It's all legal, he says, all on the up and up.

The president came on the TV and said that we have been invaded by my landlord, but not to panic, just keep a list of everything wrong. Also, to be assured, that he is working around the clock and that they have run a check on the U.S. to see if it had a previous tenant and it had, one who didn't pay one red cent, he said, so it is illegal, this exorbitant rent. Then the president spoke directly to my landlord, "Get out now, or the American people will kick your butt."

"Like I'm shaking in my boots," my landlord says. He has made it his business to know each and every one of his tenants personally. He knows what makes them tick, their ins and outs.

"I can make a rat pay rent," my landlord says, "including that one," and he turns the president off, checks to see if he has ever made a late payment, if he is behind.

The president is way behind. He will be evicted. Unless he does what my landlord says, he will be on the street. There is a new world order: my landlord.

He says he is putting all the world's trash in our backyard. He hates to throw anything out.

He says he fixed my stove; it works now.

He says my toilet is not stopped up.

He says it is not Antarctica in my apartment. He says it is the Sahara, I must be crazy. Feel this, he says, this radiator is redhot.

That leak upstairs is not a leak. The people up there are worse than stupid, he says, no matter how many times he tells them, they do not know how to take a shower right.

He set up free trade with Colombia, Thailand, and Jamaica through our storefront. Such nice boys, he says to have so many friends, to sell candy in this neighborhood, to pay so much rent, not to mention the deposit.

A few countries cannot pay rent. He turns a drip into a flood, a spark into a fire. He is insured.

He can afford to wait.

He says what happened in East Timor is none of my business. He says Haiti is no place for me to worry about. He says Miramar was on rent strike and sooner or later they're going to lose their whole building. Venezuela, too. He says if I don't like what he did in Afghanistan then why don't I just move out. He says he can do whatever he wants in Iraq. What are you going to do about it, he says. While you were watching TV, he says, he was working.

He can turn a desert into a storm. He can kill a hundred thousand and not even get a nick. There's plenty more where he came from, he says.

He is here for the long run. He knows you will cooperate. He is your new best friend, he says. He is all you got. He is living two floors down. He is spending your rent at OTB. He is absentee, but you are at home and you have begun to feel at home. You have begun to like it. You hear a knock on your door. He says you will do what he says. He is the new world order. Everything has changed overnight. Everything was rearranged while you were at work, while you were sleeping, while you were away for the summer, while you were not paying attention. He says he has thought of everything. He says he has worked it out so you don't have a choice, so you don't have to think about it. He will take care of everything. You don't have to lift a finger.

But we have begun to go behind my landlord's back. We have had meetings. We have taken a white sheet and written on it. Tomorrow we will unfurl it outside of the building, on the fire escape. The sign says rent strike. The sign says we will no longer pay for the storms in the deserts, the battles of the ships, the wars of the stars, the assaults of the land and air and sea. It says the days of the lords of the land are over, the days of the lording over, or being lorded over.

Social Security

Toward the end Bobby wore a jacket with Sherlock Holmes flaps on the shoulders. When he walked they flew up like wings.

The city feels like an ocean. Above the buildings is air. If you could break the surface maybe you could fly, which must be like moving here on the street but with less resistance.

Bobby leaves our building between B and C, floats over to Tompkins Square Park, and brings the women junkies home to his room, which is big enough for a bed. For a while he had three. "Young ones," he said with a swing of his head, up for proud, down for modest, then up again for surprise at his good luck. But one stole a hundred dollars from another and then Bobby came home to find two together in his bed. "They was just fooling me," he said, shaking his lowered head.

Bobby bobs down the street. Five steps right, stop. Five steps left, stop. Five steps catty-corner, stop.

He's thin, light, an empty glassine envelope, so when he's with his two Chihuahuas they jerk him ahead. He wears a baseball cap with a B on it and his white hair Bozo-style. His pants are short; his shoes bigger than his feet. He swings his head from side to side as though his neck is a loose coil. From a distance, it's a happy sight to see.

Me, I got my own problems here on Eleventh Street. We got gas heaters that leak. I get one pipe fixed, find another one leaking. I'm so tired. I see Bobby run up the street and I watch him and I know I should do something but I am so tired. I tell the landlady; she says I need to drink more eggnog.

If you sink here, you disappear. But then again, you might touch bottom and push off.

Bobby's got two new women. He settles on one, then another. Finally he chooses a brunette. "She's young and loves me. She wants to marry me," Bobby says, "And she don't steal from me like the blond one did. At least so far she don't."

Bobby's out with the Chihuahuas. The brunette zigzags up the street. She needs five dollars. Bad. But she looks good. Tight white pants. High heels, long hair. Up close the corners of her mouth curl downward, below her chin. Deep lines slice across wrists and forehead. Track marks on ankles, feet, arms, hands. Her head darts like her neck is the spring of a mousetrap. She stands under his window and yells, "Bobby." Maybe a hundred times.

Someone says, "Hey, he's gone."

She looks at them, then back at the window. "Bobby. Bobby. Bobby. Bobby . . ." she continues.

Here, there are only a few species: an abundance of human beings, a few dogs, an occasional horse employed by the New York Police Department, pigeons, rats, cockroaches, cats. Individual variations are surprising and beautiful; some are genetic, some store-bought, but the rats all look the same.

Bobby used to wash walls at the Bowery Hotel but is retired now. He's sixty but looks eighty on account of the missing teeth and lack of body fat. "I got lots of energy," he says. "They wanted to give me medicine to slow me down, but I said no; I like my energy. Today I walked to Forty-second Street with my honey. Fast, too."

Bobby's roommate, Frankie, turns the corner and heads up the block, slow as the tide. His body lurches one stiff step forward as though against a wave, then when it passes, he is thrown back into the open so he must juggle back and forth on his feet to get his bearings before lunging ahead again. His hand reaches forward, patting, looking for a fender to dock on. "Here comes Frankie," Bobby says, "He drinks too much."

Bobby and Frankie live two floors below me. They leave their two doors open and the smell is so bad that I take a big breath before I open the front door of the building and then try to make it at least a floor above theirs before I breathe again. There is food all over their floor. I guess for the dogs. I am an outsider. I am from Ohio. I do not know. Is this the way all of New York is? Everyone told me New York was bad, that I could never live in New York. When I come up the stairs, that's what I think, that I will never make it in New York, just like everyone said. I am sinking fast.

It's expensive to live here. Life is not cheap.

Last year, before Bobby started in with the women, he said he was a captain with the police force. He wore a red cowboy hat and stuffed his pants into red cowboy boots. "Get on little doggies," he'd say to the Chihuahuas, herding them up the steps. Bobby posted signs with Scotch tape on the fence in front of the empty lot, on light poles, and on plywood over the windows of abandoned buildings: "No Drugs, I am with Police. Member Police, Captain Bobby." On the door of the building he taped a sign, "To all who live here. do not open for woman want to see Bobby. Do not want her her. She slim. Wear blue Jean. Can walk to good. She on drug. Thank you Member police Bobby."

Bobby sits on the steps with Baby, his biggest Chihuahua. Her eyes bulge out like a frog, which is about the same size. She looks cute, cuddled in Bobby's needle-thin arms, but if anyone reaches out a hand to pet her, she growls and snaps her head. "She'll bite your hand off," Bobby says, giggling. On his door a sign says, "berare. Tack dog."

It's the first of the month, Bobby's Social Security check time. The brunette clip-clops down the steps to check the mail every three minutes. Up and down. Up and down. Then the mail carrier comes and puts the mail in the wrong boxes. The brunette bangs on the boxes, takes a bobby pin to each keyhole, then throws the bobby pin on the floor. She slides a knife under the metal boxes to jimmy them open. She shifts her weight from leg to leg. She throws her head back, sucks in a breath, then gets back to work.

"It ain't right," the neighbors say. Someone calls Social Security but the records say Bobby can handle his own money.

Frankie and Bobby fight about TV channels. Frankie wants to watch a show where each family member is an individual consumer and the home is where they come to tell jokes. Bobby wants to watch a game show where wheels spin and boxes light up. They push each other against walls, bang each other's heads against the door. Then Frankie throws the TV out the front window and Bobby calls the cops on him.

Frankie gets some, too, these women that need things. They run in and out, taking baths, doing their business, scurrying back and forth. Sometimes they are nodding out in the halls, or on the steps, leaning half over the railing, their arms dangling like corpses floating in the water.

Then Bobby tells everyone that his honey's going to have a baby. "Are you the father?" people want to know.

Bobby reckons so. He has an extra spring to his step, like someone doing water aerobics.

"But Bobby," they say, "This sounds like a line to get money, and, even so, the baby would come out all wrong since she smokes that crack."

"Don't say that," Bobby tells them, "be happy for me. I'm going to be a Daddy. Sometimes they come out all right. I hope so."

"You should take her to a rehab place," they say, "if this is true," but it wasn't.

Bobby sits on the step, craning his neck like he's trying to keep his head out of the water. "Nice night," he says. "My honey's out working. You know who much she makes? A hundred dollars. I walk up to Fourteenth Street, down to Avenue D, but I don't find her. Maybe she'll come back soon. It's nice to have a honey. Don't get so lonely."

I do not think I will last here. I can hardly stand up. I get so dizzy. Every day I look for another apartment but they are all too much money. How can we live like this: the smell of rotting plaster, the smell of urine and feces, the flies, cockroaches, mice, the bodies looking dead or like statues, slowly nodding down, the arms on the ground, the chest on the knees, the head almost to the ankles in the middle of the street. I am not sure how I will ever get off of this street. I am like flotsam on the shore, going back and forth, just on the surface, not sinking, but not landing anywhere either.

There was a man on the third floor whose face was always red. He had glasses and hair that he greased down. One day an ambulance came and they carried him out strapped to a chair. He never came back from the hospital. They said he died from alcohol. On the first floor there is a woman who I have almost seen once. She just opens the door a crack and yells for the man in the storefront. I saw blond hair. All day long, she yells for him and he comes up and then he goes and runs "errands" for her. I do not know if it is heroin or crack she does, but it must have been heroin and the man in the storefront must not have always bought her clean needles because she died. The hospital did not want to take her, but she wanted to go. They said she was discharged and they couldn't take her back. Then they took her and she didn't come back.

I think if I go I will not come back either. I have my hand up waving for help, but I think by now I am too far from shore. The deep looks so tempting, so easy.

The man in the storefront bangs all night.

"It sounds like he's hitting his head," I say to the landlady. "I think he's hurting himself down there."

"No," she says, "he's just practicing his karate, he chops bricks in half so when he goes out at night to go through trash he can protect himself. He goes all the way uptown, to the rich people's trash."

Bobby is a sitting duck. Frankie is treading water, sinking, drowning in his own blood that gurgles out of his mouth. Everyone is adrift.

Everyday there's more of them. They call up all night long. Then a man come after Frankie on account of one. Frankie sees the man everywhere. Frankie foams at the mouth. He falls down. He lunges at babies in carriages. He waves a knife in the air. An ambulance comes, ties Frankie down and takes him to the psychiatric ward, but after a while, he comes back.

Then someone rents a car and asks Frankie and Bobby if they want to go to a friend's farm upstate. The street takes a collection and a neighbor goes along to take care of them. It all happens in one day.

Bobby leaves a note on his door. "Honey, I can't stand it. I move out. I can't take it anymore."

Me, I am still here, treading water, bobbing in the waves, trying to keep my head up, to catch my breath, to not go down a third time, but I am afraid the truth is is that I am sinking fast.

Zenith

It was 1962, the year of symbols. Knowing all the words to songs meant you were neat. Wearing wedgie shoes meant you were cool. Wearing hose meant you were sophisticated. Having a boy's ring meant you were going steady and wrapping it in angora and wearing it on a chain around your neck meant everything in the world.

I wore orthopedic saddle shoes. I wore white socks. I didn't even know all the words to "Duke of Earl." I would have gone steady with Donald Bickle, the creepiest boy in the whole school, but when I sent him notes ("You're nice. I like you. Do you like me?"), he would lift them off his desk with two fingers, hold them away from him and make a big to-do about not breathing until he dropped them in the wastebasket by the teacher's desk.

"What was that?" Mrs. Walker would ask.

"Nothing," Donald would say.

"Then why did you have to disturb the class to throw it away?"

"It was snot," he'd say, looking down at his feet. "I forgot to bring a Kleenex." On the way back to his desk, he'd make a fart noise when he'd pass me.

Everything was a symbol and I didn't have any of my own. Then my brother, out of nowhere, got a transistor radio. Having a transistor radio, I thought, would be better than having Sputnik in your backyard, a horse you could keep in your garage, or free rides forever on the roller coaster at Meyers Lake Amusement Park.

"Wow," I said, "can I borrow it sometime?" Now I could finally learn all the words to "Walk on By," and "Return to Sender." I could take it to the playground and get a boyfriend, no problem. Suddenly the transistor radio became a symbol for my entire future. My whole life would be an unchained melody with me singing it. My life would be in perfect syncopation. It would be me going loop de loop, loop de lie.

My brother was polishing the front of the radio with a handkerchief. He wears glasses and white shirts, is an Eagle Scout, plays in the band and is popular at church, the Church of the Brethren.

He's sitting at his desk and I'm standing at the door because I'm not allowed in.

"Borrow it?" He looks up, surprised-like.

"I just want to hear what it sounds like. I won't even take it off the porch. Promise."

"Do you think I'm going to let my grimy-handed sister TOUCH my transistor radio?"

"I'll wash my hands. I'll wash my whole body. I'll take a bath with soap. Comet. Clorox. You name it."

"Battery acid and boiling water," he says and slams the door.

I go down to the basement. My mother is feeding clothes into the wringers, which are set up between two gray metal tubs. The clothes tongue out between the rollers like a flat board and underneath water gushes out of a porcelain scoop like a gray waterfall. Fifteen piles of clothes arranged by color are scattered on the cement floor.

"First a BB gun and now a transistor radio." I say. "Where'd Arnold get a transistor radio?" I stand in the middle of the basement floor rigid as though I'm on the edge of a high dive.

"Uncle Bob got it for him." Uncle Bob is my mother's friend's husband.

"Do you think Uncle Bob would get me one?"

"Of course not. Arnold WORKS for Uncle Bob."

"Could I work for Uncle Bob?"

"At a garage?"

"I want to work for Uncle Bob. I want a transistor radio," I say.

"You want to work? That'd be the day."

Then I remember why I never come to the basement when my mother is washing clothes. First she's going to make the clothes get stuck in the rollers. Then she's going to put her hand in so it gets stuck. Then she's going to run upstairs and lock me down here to do the wash. I look at the piles of clothes. I should go upstairs right now, I think.

"First he gets a BB gun and now a transistor radio," I scream.

My mother starts the rollers going backward so some of the clothes will get stuck.

"I want a transistor radio," I scream.

She starts the rollers going again and some of the clothes go around and around, plastered to the rollers.

"He gets new clothes and I have to wear Donna Jean's stupid hand-me-downs."

My mother starts tugging at the wad of clothes.

"I hate Donna Jean's polka-dotted dresses and orthopedic shoes," I yell.

My mother turns the machine on and off. On and off.

"He has a racing bike and all I have is a fat-tire bike that the chain falls off of all the time."

My mother is tugging at the wad of clothes.

"And now he has a TRANSISTOR RADIO." Just when I get to the TRAN part she does it. She puts her hand between the rollers and lets it go in. The machine stops with a big clang and she pulls her hand out and holds it up to the light bulb above the sinks.

"Now look what you made me do," she says.

"He got to go to camp, too," I scream.

"After all I've done for you. Look what you made me do. It's BROKEN." She bends over and, squatting, runs to the basement steps.

"He has penny loafers." I say.

"You finish the wash. I have to go to the HOSPITAL." She stomps up the steps, slams the door and locks it. I sit on the bale of straw my mother's last boyfriend bought for Arnold's BB practice. The same boyfriend that promised me a horse from his farm in Kentucky.

Now she's going to call her friends, I think. I walk over to the heater vent and hear my mother dialing the phone.

"You'll never guess what she did this time. Here I am raising these kids ALONE," I hear.

I crawl up on the table that is stacked with every *Canton Repository* newspaper back to 1956. I scramble out of the little basement window, squinting, into the dappled light. I run in the narrow space between our house and our neighbor's, stomp past my brother on the porch listening to "Make It Easy on Yourself," the transistor to his ear, open the screen door so it bangs against the house, and pound up the steps.

"Where do you think you're going?" my mother says, hand over the phone.

"There was something wrong with her from the moment she was born," she says back into the phone. "She was born MENTALLY ILL."

I should leave now, I think, but Arnold has blocked the door. I should keep my mouth shut and go up to my room and lock the door.

"Go break your hand," I say, "then stick it up your asshole." I stand halfway up the steps. I know what happens next.

Years later my mother, helpless as my houseguest, hundreds of miles away from her home, would say, "You know I was afraid of you." I know she thinks I should apologize for the brat I was.

"You blew it now," Arnold says, standing by my mother at the phone.

"Look," my mother says into the phone, "she's at it again. I'll call you right back, okay?"

"Dickhead," I scream and bound up the steps, three at a time, using my hands to propel me. At the top I make the wrong choice and head to my room, close the door and lock it with my foot, but Arnold is there too soon and forces his arm through the door. He latches onto my hair. He falters and I slam the door on his arm but lose my footing and then he's in and has me down, one hand pulling my hair, the other has my arm behind my back. We kick, scratch, push, fall, stomp, knock over furniture until I get free and run to the bathroom fast enough to get the lock fastened. He bangs on the door. I am safe.

"Hear this?" he says and I hear glass breaking on the floor outside the bathroom door.

"It's your glass horse. I'm breaking everything in your room until you come out."

"Go ahead," I say.

I hear my mother come up the steps. "Oh Arnold," she says, "I don't know what I'd do without you."

Four days later I get my chance and take it. I'm in my room working on my book. It's about a stray dog who runs away from home and is picked up by the dogcatcher but gets free. The dog's name is Joe-Joe and he's on a journey to find the perfect home. It starts out like *Black Beauty*, the middle is like *Lassie Come Home*, except Joe-Joe gets to see his old owner burn in a forest fire like in *Bambi*, and it ends up like *Old Yeller*. I'm almost to the end. *Joe-Joe's mouth is foaming. Joe-Joe is angry*, I write, *But Joe-Joe still has not found the perfect home. Will anyone take him like this? Joe-Joe wipes his mouth on the grass, walks up to the cabin. He sees a nice man chopping wood. Joe-Joe tries to act cute like when he was a puppy but instead of a yap yap, Joe-Joe hears himself snarling, snarling, growling like a dog with rabies. Don't give up Joe-Joe. Things will get better.*

I reread what I've written. I cross out "will" and put "might."

My brother clicks by my door in his Eagle Scout uniform and cleats. He runs down the steps and out the door. I lean out the window and watch him until I see him cross at the corner of Dougherty and Fulton. Then I open his door. Pencils are lined up on his desk. His lime-green chenille bedspread is tucked in around his pillows. His dresser drawers are all pushed in. On one side of the dresser is his iron piggy bank. I take a penny out of my pocket and turn the screw. It falls open into two pieces. I take out three quarters and four dimes and put back six pennies for weight. I screw the pig back together and put it back in its exact spot.

On the other side is the transistor radio sitting up by its brass stand. I know I am about to steal it. It is 5" x 8" x 1 ½". It is made of maroon plastic with a round brass speaker on the front above which the letters Z E N I T H are perfectly spaced. Across the top a brass band had two maroon dials. Then one on the left has OFF and VOLUME circling it. The one on the right has 14 ˆ 10 8 7 ˆ 6 5 around it. It looks like a face with the speaker as a mouth and the dials as eyes. In the center of the dials (a nose) stands a coat of arms–type emblem with a three-pronged crown, a lightning Z in the center, and an earth with stars to the right and one lone star to the left.

I pick it up. I reach for the dial and pretend I'm John Glenn about to pull the switch that will send me out of Cape Canaveral, out of Florida, away from Earth and into orbit. I hear a song about a guy being a rebel and never, ever being any good and that even though he doesn't do what everyone else does, that doesn't mean that she doesn't love him. I hear footsteps on the porch and the screen door slam. I turn off the dial and tiptoe out of the room. I slip the radio under my T-shirt and hold it against my ribs with my arm. I run down the steps, out the door, and to the bushes in the backyard. I crawl under them and into the house I made out of twigs. I turn the dial. I hear a song about wanting to be Bobby's girl. I hear "Monster Mash," "Soldier Boy," and "Breaking Up Is Hard to Do." I hear a song about coming out tonight.

Then I remember I don't have much time before Arnold gets back. I stick the radio under my shirt and in my pants and hold it with my arm while I run to the Summit School playground.

Everyone is there. Jean, Linda, Sue, Chris, the popular girls, are sitting on the school steps. Bill, Matt, Jimmy, Tony, and Dave, the popular boys, are skateboarding down the hill. I switch on the dial and lean on the fence. Instead of "Twist and Shout," like I want, stupid Bobby Vinton is singing that roses are red and violets are blue. I'm afraid to switch the dial. I'm afraid I won't be able to find the same station and then Arnold will know I took the radio. The song goes on and on.

"Hi Sandy," Linda says. Linda has never said hi to me before.

"Oh, hi," I say.

"What's that?" Debbie asks.

"My transistor radio. I just got it. I hate Bobby Vinton, don't you?"

Bill and Matt walk over. They all crowd around me. Now they will see now wonderful I am, I think. Now they will want me to sit at their table at the Big Wedge. Now they will let me be part of the whip at the ice skating pond. Now boys will try to go steady with me just to be with me, Sandy, a popular girl.

"Here, I'll switch the channel," Linda says and takes the radio. She turns to a twistin' song, about twistin' the night away. They all start dancing. I join in but they make a circle around Linda. Then Matt takes the radio and comes over and dances with me. Soon everyone is around us and we're all dancing.

"Hey, Sandy can dance," Matt says. Then commercials come on and we wander over to sit on the steps. They let me be in the center. I try to find the station where my brother had it set.

"I gotta go," I say, switching the radio off.

"Can you leave the radio? We'll bring it by your house," Linda says.

"Just go and come right back," Matt says, "We'll keep the radio."

"I'll take it home and bring it to school tomorrow. Okay, Sandy?"

"No," I say, "I gotta go and take the radio."

"Just one more song, then," Bill says. He grabs the radio and turns it on. "The Locomotion" comes on and they all form a chain with Bill at the front.

"We're just going to dance around the school then we'll be right back," Bill says. Then Bill leads them down the hill and back behind the school. I sit down on the steps. I should have gone with them, I think. I should have led the chain when I heard "Locomotion" come on. Then I would tell them why I can't go home late, why I can't go home at all. Maybe Linda would take me home with her and her family would adopt me. They'd buy me nice clothes and I would sit around with their family, eat popcorn and watch TV. A mosquito bites me. Oh, no, I think, that means it must be 9:00. Arnold gets home at 9:15, so I run around the school but they aren't there. I run all around the building but I can't find them. I run to Linda's house but the lights are all off.

I run to the Big Wedge on Twelfth Street and look in the window but they aren't there, either. Maybe they went to Chris's to show her the radio, I think, and I run down to her house by the park. I ring her bell but her father tells me she's studying. I cross the street to the train tracks. The sky is orange and I can hardly see the railroad ties to walk on them. By now my brother has come home, has told my mother and both of them are waiting, locked together in looking down the street for me.

I can't go home.

I jump over the railroad tracks and walk over to the stream. The same stream that I sailed my raft on two years ago. The raft I thought would carry me out of Canton, Ohio, to the Tuscarawas River, to the Ohio River, to the Mississippi River, and then to an island in the Pacific Ocean. The same raft that along with a junk car and twenty fifty-five-gallon drums is rotting away in the viaduct under the Tuscarawas Boulevard.

I cross the creek and head over to the McKinley Memorial. One hundred and eight marble steps lead up to the dome-shaped building and I take them, two at a time, without missing a beat. At the top, I run, around and around the monument. The sky is blue, the color of Pelican ink, then troll-doll-hair orange; the trees are black; the marble is like snow in the spotlights and around and around I go, like Man o' War, the greatest racer of all. I break through the wire, the winner.

I sit at the top of the steps and look down on the green statue of McKinley. He was a kid, just like me, I think. He probably had a million brothers and sisters. A person who became president of the United States and then got assassinated probably lived in one of the houses that I can see. He probably took his brother's electric train and broke it. Or his sister's bicycle with the big front wheel. His mother probably told him that he was born with something wrong with him, that he was born bad and that he wouldn't amount to anything, that he wasn't worth the food he ate. She probably told him that she was going to dump him off forever at the orphanage.

I looked at the rooftops and tried to find mine. I pretended it was the future and that I was a little girl who had found the rooftop of that famous person, Sandy Ward, who became an astronaut and flew, floating in perfect weightlessness, to the planet Venus where she discovered the special food that saved Earth from total destruction. Sandy Ward, who bought the Space Needle in Seattle, closed the revolving restaurant, and made it into her private home.

Sandy Ward, who was once a nobody in Canton, Ohio.

The lights went off and everything was pitch black. I walked down the steps, out of the park, and home. I went in the kitchen and ate three bowls of Cheerios and one bowl of Wheaties. I went up to my room and started on page 268 of Joe-Joe's story, *The nice man was chopping wood. He put down his ax and bent over to pet Joe-Joe. He was sad and lonely and always wanted a dog. Joe-Joe wanted to lick his hand but he bit him instead. He couldn't stop himself. Joe-Joe snarled and foamed at the mouth. "Easy there, Buddy," the man said, "Take it easy."*

After a while I heard the screen door slam. "She's home," Arnold said and started up the steps.

It all turned out pretty bad in the end.

Then, twenty-six years later, when I'm not a famous astronaut but starting to accept being Sandy Ward, when it is way past the time that I'd stopped being the person Arnold or my mother wanted me to be, when it was at least a year past the time I stopped hurting myself quite so badly, I am walking down First Avenue in New York and spot, mixed in with a street person's wares, a maroon Zenith transistor radio.

I point to it, gasp. The homeless man is leaning on the parking meter, his arm on the top of it, his head flipping back and forth while he scratches his neck under his shirt.

"It's the first one ever made," the man says, dancing in his dirty tennis shoes around his books, his old records, his half empty bottles of perfume, and a purse. Bending down, he picks up the radio.

"I'll take it," I say.

"Listen," he says and he turns the dial from OFF to the U. "It works just fine."

And there it is, a song about loop de looping, loop de lying.

I tell him the story of my brother, the other Zenith, while I search for my money, pay. "I'll give it to him for a Christmas present," I say, thinking that that is the only way I can justify buying it, not wanting the homeless person to think I am buying it for myself, that I am selfish.

"My, my," the homeless man says, brightening. He puts the money in his front pocket, pulls a rag out of his back pocket, wipes the radio, looks down at me, puts his hand on my shoulder. "That shows progress. Maturity. Real growth. I'm glad I could be a part."

I can tell he doesn't believe me for a minute. I grab the Zenith, run fast to the corner, then turn onto Ninth Street, out of his sight. Truth was I never touched Arnold's radio. I just told the story to try to be someone I am really not, someone that acts, instead of is acted on, someone more feisty, more pushy. Arnold probably still has his Zenith, I think. He doesn't need two. No, I decide that finding this Zenith is a symbol, a symbol that things I want will come to me. So that I can stop thinking everyone else has to have something before I can. So that I can stop thinking it is wrong to want.

I'm keeping this one, I think, but if I ever find another one, and I hope I do, then I'll give that one to Arnold, first thing.

All for One and One for All

All this happened when I was a bigger liar than I am now. The
setting is Canton, Ohio, in the early sixties. Picture steel mills:
green buildings several blocks long, lit up at night by metal pouring down like lava inside. Picture two-story wooden houses built
for the factory workers and just ten years from being condemned.
Picture a downtown before all the stores moved out to the suburbs. And picture me: fat with blond, ratted hair, blotchy skin, and
wearing a straight skirt rolled up at the waist to make a mini and a
long mohair sweater.

I'm twelve, at my prime in the lying category, and capable of
changing Time, Space, Energy, and Matter with words. With
adults I lied about where I was, who I was with, where I got what
I had, what time it was if I snuck sock-footed home late. With my
peers it was more difficult. Only the younger ones believed, I think
now. But I still lied. About Jimmy Kendall having a crush on me.
About how many Motown records I had. Mostly, though, I lied
about my father.

When we all wanted a horse, my father lived out west and
owned a ranch. When the Beatles came out, my father was in Lon-
don arranging all their tours. When Kennedy got shot, my father
was in the car right behind him and got shot in the kneecap. My
father was a rich businessman. A doctor. The only survivor of
Buddy Holly's plane crash. A poet, musician, and ventriloquist.
He owned four stores downtown.

"Did you see Ed Sullivan last night?" I'd ask my best friend
Debbie on the way home from school.

"No, I missed it."

"Oh, man, how could you? My father was on last night. He's
a comedian now and God was he funny. Ed Sullivan said he was
'A really big show, a really big show.' Just like that," I said, loud
enough for everyone around to hear.

"Wow, that's really keen," Debbie said.

Friends were like that about lies. Nancy Farley's brother went to jail for killing her stepfather by knocking his head seventeen times against the kitchen sink. That year at her birthday party we sat at the kitchen table and ate ice cream and cake and never once looked at the sink or the floor around it.

"My brother got a job in Hollywood as an actor," she said.

"Neat," we all said, "will he be on TV?"

There were two groups. All the Downtowners, which is what we called ours, were at the party. The seven of us were inseparable: Debbie, Nancy, Sherry, Linda, Susie, Mary Lou and me. We started out running through water hoses in underpants and went right up through pedal pushers to frayed jeans and miniskirts. We read *Mad Magazine*, played step ball and kick the can, hypnotized each other, had séances, giggled all night at pajama parties, asked important questions of the magic eight ball and Ouija board, sang "Town without Pity," a capella, drank Cokes and ate buttered French fries at the Big Wedge, our hangout. Mostly we pretended we were middle class and respected each other's lies like they were a brand-new 45. Lying was our bread and butter and our salvation. We started out with nothing, threw in some lies, and came up with pure and glorious Power, which we were all into that year. Lies could give us wealth, create famous relatives, take us to Disneyland and back, turn hand-me-downs into store-bought clothes, make week-old runs in hose happen just that day, and give us fathers.

The second group, the Cake-eaters, lived in a neighborhood ten blocks away with big painted houses, grass on the lawns, trees, and two parents. Sometimes at school we copied things they said, like: "My parents won't let me," "In the rec room," "My dance lessons," or "I have to go home for dinner."

There were moments of perfect truth, though. Like the time I beat out Ricky Franklin, the leader of the Cake-eaters, and won the public school art contest. And then turned right around and won the Summit School Scholar of the Year Award. When the teacher announced it to the class I was hoping all the Cake-eaters were feeling as bad as I was good, when Ricky said loud enough for the whole class to hear, "If she's such a smart shit then why does she put more Kleenex in the right side of her bra than the left side?" And there I was, wearing a tight sweater. I folded my arms over my chest and didn't move them until I got in the cloakroom and tore into Ricky. I punched him in the stomach. Grabbed his shirt and ripped it, pushing him into the galoshes in the corner. He got up swinging and smacked me against the coat hooks. He pulled my hair and I jammed my hand flat into his face before everybody screaming "fight, fight" brought the teacher and the principal.

He looked pathetic in the principal's office with his head tilted back and holding that bloody piece of cotton on his nose. "I'm going to smash your face to smithereens, Sandy Ward," he said. I raised my eyebrows, cocked my head to the side, smoothed out my skirt, and clicked my tongue against my teeth.

I shouldn't have been so smug. Anyone could tell it wasn't a fair fight. I was the tallest one in the class and weighed a good twenty pounds more than Ricky. He must have started lifting weights, because the next time we got into it, it got ugly. It all started when he called Linda's mother a crazy bat.

Linda's father had died the year before and Linda's mother had taken to wandering and screaming undressed in the streets at night. Once she walked naked all the way to Lemmon's Grocery and filled a whole cart before the police came. Linda wouldn't play the Ouija board or let herself be hypnotized at pajama parties anymore.

"Your mother's a loony case, Linda Edwards, and my parents say you'll turn out the same way," Ricky said on the way downtown after school.

"You're dead, Ricky," I said. I threw my books down and already I could hear people yelling "fight, fight" and running our way. I pushed his shoulder and stood back waiting for him to try to hit so I could get him one in the face. He jumped around like Cassius Clay and I faked a right and went for left when the next thing I knew my arm was behind me, my face was on the pavement, and his foot was on my neck.

"Say uncle," he said. I did. As soon as I was up, I kicked him in the leg and smacked the back of his head before I took off. I'm fighting dirty from now on, I told myself, and I'm lying about saying uncle.

Everybody lied. My mother, a schoolteacher, lied about what she did, where she'd go on Friday nights and Sunday afternoons. I didn't see her come home, but others did. "Mrs. Ward is a whore, Mrs. Ward is a whore," they'd singsong. If you knew my mother, you'd think it was funny, too.

My mother was what they then called a divorcee, who raised three children alone. "At least I never took welfare," she'd say, "we'll starve first," and we did. Morning, noon, and night we ate the expired cereal that my brother-in-law got free from his job. I always suspected she wanted to desert us and go off around the world, or to the Riviera, or Paris, or somewhere, anywhere else.

Mary Lou's mom was on welfare. They had powdered milk, cheese, and canned food with white labels. Sometimes when I was walking in the alley, I would see her mom in the leaves, under the bushes. Made me jump. Man, I'd think, I thought I was alone. Later, I learned she was drunk. Mary Lou's dad was in jail, and her two older sisters, who were in the ninth grade, were in charge of the eight kids. One sister had a baby of her own. Mary Lou always had the baby on her arm. "I'm the luckiest person in the world," she'd lie, "Isn't she the cutest?" Her dad, she said, was on tour. "He's Evil Knievel," she said, "that's why he has all those tattoos."

"Keen," we said.

I passed the school year wanting Jimmy Kendall to like me. He was tall and thin with thick brown hair and Beatle boots, which I coveted. I thought he was the most beautiful boy alive. I'd sit at my desk and look at the back of his head two seats in front of me and think about kissing him. I'd never been kissed but I'd read about it in a book Nancy had and those words, which I memorized, I repeated to myself. I would be leaning against a wall holding my books. Jimmy would walk up to me and lean his shoulder against the wall and face me. First we would talk about school and then he would say, "I like you, Sandy," and I would look up and he would bend down and kiss me. I would drop my books and put my arms around his shoulders and he would lean toward me and I would kiss his neck and he would kiss mine. It would feel like the time he brushed my hand in the cloakroom only even stronger. Like fireworks, the book said. I'd spend the day with flushed cheeks working myself up into quite a state with various renditions of this dream. It was a lovely school year.

It was my mother who ended what I still consider to be my most perfect relationship. I'm walking back from downtown on Market and Jimmy Kendall is walking toward me on Twelfth. On the corner we fall in together.

"I love your Beatle boots," I think but can't say. They're too large and scuffle on the sidewalk. It is cold, in March, and neither of us have heavy coats.

Truth is we don't say a word, just glide on together down Twelfth, past the gay bar, past Martin's Pastry Shop, past Lemmon's Grocery, and past the huge mansion, which I think is now a vacant lot, or a porno video place, which is what almost all the buildings in my old neighborhood are now. We walk up to the porch, which encircles the entire mansion. I pull a board off the back of a bay window and we crawl in. He follows me to the dark, wood dining room, then his eyes follow mine to the chandelier gleaming in the dark. We move through the rooms separately, though I can hear him on the circular stairway or see him through a doorway. We touch the same wood, the same stained glass, the same trunk in the attic, the same yellow dress inside. We crawl back through the window and I replace the board. We walk to my house.

Inside we kneel and put our hands over the radiator. We kiss. I lean back and he follows me. I open my mouth. I open my legs. I open my chest. Then the door bangs open against our legs and cold air hits us. My mother stands with a bag of groceries.

"Out," she screams at Jimmy. "Out. Out. Out." She points toward the door and Jimmy, Beatle boots dragging, slouches out.

"One hour," she tells me. "You have one hour to pack for your sister's."

My sister, Jane, and her husband, Mark, lived in the suburbs and had three children. She was pregnant. She saw me standing on the curb with my boxes and she thought, here comes my built-in babysitter. Which was okay with me because at the same time I was thinking that finally, no lie, I was going to see what being a Cake-eater was all about. My sister had a house with a lawn in the suburbs. But I soon learned why on holidays, my mother used to say, "Leave your brother-in-law alone. Don't make him mad."

He beat my sister up. Next morning she would pretend like nothing happened. I even got in the habit of tensing up and acting sheepish when he was around, just like she did. Like one wrong move and that would be it. Lights out forever. He broke her nose once but my sister's still with him. "I'm never leaving the suburbs," she said. My sister was never going to have her children be Downtowners. She was never going to be a Downtowner, no way. My sister looked just like me, only pretty, and Mark was a big guy, an ex-football player and fraternity member from Ohio State, where they met. He'd tell jokes and we'd all laugh.

"Who's your favorite brother-in-law?" he'd say.

"You are," I'd answer.

"That a girl." Then he'd slap me on the back and turn to Jane, who was clearing the dishes. This is how you deal with creeps like this, she taught me: act busy. "Your sister here is smart, real smart. She's going to go places."

I wanted to go places. Like right back to Canton, the Downtowners, and Jimmy Kendall. Downtown was where there were bright lights, all waiting for me. I was seeing a whole new twilight zone of lies. It put a taint on lying for me thereafter. I didn't have my heart in it.

Living in the suburbs wasn't so great. Everybody had two parents, but it wasn't all it's cracked up to be, I saw. The dads weren't actually around, for one thing. My friend Pat's dad was around all the time because he was not working and it was her mom that worked at a factory making plastic toys at night. Melanie's dad used to be a tool and die engineer, but now he was selling chemicals and cleaning stuff, and he would go out on the road for weeks and sometimes not even make any money. Bonnie's dad had bad nerves, she said, which really meant he was mean because he got drunk so we couldn't go over to her house. Pat's refrigerator was always empty. Just milk and pickles. She said they were going to lose their house and would have to move downtown.

"It's not so bad downtown," I told her, "it's way neater, honest." The worst part about the suburbs was you couldn't go anywhere. My sister was home all day and all night without a car. If we wanted to go anywhere, we had to beg someone's mom for a ride. Downtown, I explained to Pat, was better on account of you could walk everywhere. In Canton in the winter, you could skate on the creeks to a whole new neighborhood. You could go to the Italian neighborhood, the Greek neighborhood, the projects. You could walk to the big stone library downtown and try to find out about another city, another life, another place entirely.

I promised myself instead of lying I was going to find out about the truth.

"You're homesick," Jane said when I left.

"Yeah, I guess that's it," I said.

"I enjoyed having you here."

"I liked being here. Wish I could stay longer," I lied.

When I got back Jimmy Kendall was gone. Another one of the factories closed and that was the end of the Kendall family. Now the Beatle boots were gone forever.

It didn't bother me, I told myself, because it was spring and time to start the festival. Every year I organized a festival in the vacant lot across the alley from my backyard and all the Downtowners helped. Mary Lou promised to do the Haunted House because we all thought it might be too gory for Nancy, who used to do it before the murder. This was the first year we were going to have a dance. The Echoes, the best band in town, agreed to play. We made posters, put them up, and went door-to-door collecting prizes.

"This is going to be the best one yet," Debbie said as we dragged the bathtub we had found in the alley into the lot.

She was right. We sold popcorn, Kool-Aid, Cokes, candy, and brownies. There was a go-fish game, a ringtoss, a dog show, a throw-the-pennies-into-Coke-bottles game, and a hit-the-balloons-with-darts game. All with prizes. People from neighborhoods we never even heard of came. They screamed in the haunted house. They squealed and clapped their hands when they'd catch a fish. Judy D'Angelo won the hula-hoop contest and went right on without letting it drop for a whole half an hour after the contest was over. Susie's older brother, who had a horse at the fairgrounds, rode it through the streets with a sign advertising the festival. Then he came and gave kids free rides. I was in my kitchen making popcorn and putting it in little paper bags. Even my mother helped with the popcorn. She'd take it out and get to talking to the adults, who were having as much fun as everyone else.

The dance was the best part. We ran an extension cord from the gas station and made lanterns out of Christmas lights and paper bags. A band. A real band. We didn't even mind when Nick Vinnelli drum-soloed for his usual forty-five minutes. Debbie, Sherry, Linda, Susie, Nancy, Mary Lou, and I had routines worked out where we danced in a line and turned all at the same time. We felt so popular, what with everyone from school being there. Albert Garcia asked me to slow dance. And I did the Mashed Potatoes with Matt DeFore, the most popular boy in the whole school. I heard Ricky showed up but I didn't even see him. The lot was a mass of dancers. Doing the Pony, the Twist, and the Locomotion. We even had a Limbo bar. It was, I think now, the best night of my entire life.

Next day we cleaned up and then counted the money. My dining room table was stacked with piles of dimes, nickels, quarters, and dollars.

"We're rich," Sherry said.

"Shhh," Debbie said, "twenty-nine, thirty, thirty-one, thirty-two . . ."

"How much is it?"

I was putting the numbers down. "One hundred sixty-seven dollars and nine cents. Twenty-three dollars and eighty-seven cents each," I said. We looked at each other, our hands still on our piles of money in front of us, and it was like the dining room table became a huge Ouija pointer and we were all connected and seeing some power between us even better than lying.

"This is just the beginning," Linda said.

"Just the beginning," I repeated.

"All for one, and one for all," Debbie said. "All for one, and one for all," we said over and over again, louder and louder in a song.

"Let's divide the money and go down to Sam's Carry-Out to change it into dollars," Sherry said.

"Then we'll go to the Big Wedge and celebrate," Debbie said.

Sam was glad to get the change. "You girls made big moolah," he said and gave us each a bottled Coke and toasted to our success: "To the Downtowners and the Sixth Street festival."

"Let's still go to the Big Wedge," Nancy said. On the way we ran into Ricky and his friends. He stopped us and I thought he was going to say, "What a party last night," but he didn't.

"Sandy," he said, "I've got something very serious to tell you."

"Spit it out, asshole."

"Your father's name is Donald Ward, isn't it?"

Whenever I asked my mother about my father, she'd say, "I don't want to say anything negative, so I'm not going to say anything all." I wouldn't have known my father's name if I hadn't seen it on some luggage in the attic.

"Maybe it is and maybe it's not," I said.

"My dad says that's your dad's name. My dad's the judge and he sees your dad once a week," he said. "For being drunk, or stealing, or getting in a fight. If he's not in jail, he's downtown somewhere asleep on the sidewalk. Some famous dad you got there, Sandy Ward."

"So what," I said, "so what." I guess my fistfighting days were over because I didn't want to hit Ricky or anyone else ever again.

"This is going to be the best hamburger and French fries I ever had," I said as we went into the Big Wedge. "Sugar Shack" was playing on the jukebox, our favorite table was empty, all my friends were there, and we had wads of dollar bills.

"In the street," I said, "Next year we'll have the festival in the street."

"We'll tear it up. Blockade it off," Susie said.

"Out of the dirt and into the street," Nancy said.

"It will be ours. All ours," Debbie said.

My Sister

My sister moves from room to room, around and around her house, saying something I cannot understand. Something hard and sharp. I go to the top of the stairs, bend down. I hear *didn't*. I hear *don't*. I hear *won't*, *can't*.

"Yes, I'm here," I yell, "are you calling me?"

She has come around the corner, her arms folded across her chest. She is bent over. "No," she says, "I was just talking to myself."

"Okay," I say.

My sister talks to me like I am an adult. I'm fourteen. I try to talk back like an adult. It makes me feel like I can do anything.

My mother just dumped me here on my sister. I know my mom is not giving her any support for me. I try to do my part. I try to do things even before I'm asked. All the jobs no one would want to do. When my sister gives me advice, I listen.

"You know gold is really a good investment," my sister says. She tells me what I should buy, what I am supposed to like, what has value, and what doesn't. She tells me that having money, having a big house, getting away from our mother, having a living room where no one goes and a family room with a TV are the most important things of all. We are bent into each other, folding diapers in threes for toddlers, in fours for infants.

I nod.

"My children will not be raised by a single parent, no matter what," she says.

I nod. Our mom is a single parent. She moved away from our father, who was a big drinker. I have no memory of him.

"I'm never going to have children, not ever," I say, but that part is not true. The next year I had a baby girl.

After my grown-up talk, I go back to my chemistry. I have four hours of homework a night. I do it. I am keeping up. I want to go somewhere good, to the best place I can. My sister goes back to her walking and talking. She is waiting for my brother-in-law to come home.

Here's what happens then: he wants to see my nephew's homework. My nephew is not doing well in the first grade. Then I hear my brother-in-law come up the stairs. He goes to my nephew's room and wakes him. Then I hear my nephew's nub-bottomed pajama feet follow him down the steps.

Next: "Two and two is what?" my brother-in-law says. His hand slaps down hard on the table. I hear a chair fall on its side. I hear my nephew scream. I hear him being slapped on the side of the head. Then I hear, "What is two and two?" again.

I am already on history. I have two more subjects to go. My sister is walking up the stairs now. Her bedroom door closes. I do not hear her talking.

What I want I saw six years ago when I was nine, but I am not telling anyone. It was at my sister's house. A barbecue. Guests were coming. When they arrived, I saw they were a white-haired woman and man, wearing jeans and blue work shirts. They had construction boots on, both of them.

"Have some drinks," my brother-in-law said, but they declined.

"Have a drink," he said to me, then laughed.

"I don't know what is wrong with your sister," he said to my sister, "she doesn't want a drink."

Then the guests showed slides of their walk across Africa after they had finished their time in the Peace Corps. They were eighty, they said, but there they were in their backpacks and bandanas, their smiles, squinting at us, with sand dunes behind.

"I want to be like them," I said to myself, "I want to be like them."

My sister tells me that this is my dream come true. To live here in the suburbs instead of downtown with my mother. There, I was poor. Here, I am at the rich school. Before I came here, I never heard of Columbia or Berkeley. I want to be a famous journalist, writer, artist. I want to walk across Africa. I want to go to France.

"France, schmance," my brother-in-law says. He has grabbed my arm. He is holding it behind my back. He is bending me down, putting his legs around mine so I fall. Then he holds my face down on the floor with his knee while he tickles me or spanks me. I am supposed to say uncle.

"Don't talk back. Be nice," my mother used to say. My mother takes her green and black pills, barbiturates. When I used to fill her prescription at the drugstore, the pharmacist would walk over and ask me to come to the side. "Are you all right?" he wants to know. I nod. I am always polite to adults. "This is enough to knock over a mule," he says.

"Thank you," I say and take the prescription.

My mother says what is wrong with my sister and me is that we never look on the bright side of things.

When my brother-in-law comes home, I hear the ice clinking in the glass. My sister doesn't talk, except to say, "Yes," or "That's right."

Me, I am up in my room, making equations, taking notes.

Every night my brother-in-law gives my nephew, the one that was born a genius, a lesson.

One thing I forgot to say about the way my brother-in-law tickles me. Some of the time he misses my stomach. I try to squirm away. He catches me again.

"Say uncle," he says. I am in a choke hold or being dragged around while he holds my head in the crook of his arm.

At school, my teachers ask me if I am going to college.

"Of course," I say.

My sister says I can't go to Columbia. She says I should live at home with her and go to practical nursing school.

"I can't go to college?" I ask.

"I don't see how."

"You should go to the University of Pittsburgh if you want to stay at home," my chemistry teacher says, "It's a good school."

"Okay," I say.

My sister is going to the hospital to have her fourth baby. She is standing out on the lawn with her suitcase. I am inside with the kids. A neighbor will take her to the hospital.

While she is gone, my brother-in-law holds me down, grabs my breasts. He looks at me in the eye. He is not pretending to tickle me anymore. He is not pretending to wrestle. After, I go up to my room and lock the door.

My new niece cries all day, all night. I can hold her in one hand but her voice fills up this whole house, goes down the hill, across the street. She will not stop crying.

The next time I hear my nephew's nub-bottomed pajama feet on the steps at night, I go over to the landing. "How do you spell cat," my brother-in-law says. My nephew is taking in short breaths, trying to hold down a cry, trying to make a sound as sweet as *see*, as I. What comes up with the sound of *see* is a cry, too. He cannot stop it.

I hear the slap on the side of the head; I hear the chair fall over, more slaps.

I tiptoe down the steps. I walk down the hall and look in the kitchen. My nephew has his hands over his head. My brother-in-law is standing up, slapping him, yelling, "See, see, see." My sister is in the room behind, in the dark. Her hands are folded over her chest. She is smoking a cigarette.

"Stop," I say, "Stop." My brother-in-law turns and looks at me, then turns back to hitting my nephew.

I pick up a chair, quiet, then I hold it over his head and I bring it down, hard. It breaks over his back.

He turns, slow, and looks at me. He says, "You can't do that."

"Yes, I can." I say, "I just did." I pick up another chair. Then he turns and goes out the door. I hear him go up the stairs and my sister follow him.

I pick up my nephew and hold him. I take him up to his bed, brush his hair back from his forehead until he falls asleep.

Next day, I am using a toothbrush and Comet to clean between the tiles in the bathroom. My sister comes to the door, says that I better pack, that I have to go.

"Where?" I say.

"You know where," she says, "to mother."

My sister was on the debate team at her college. She stood straight and tall. Her voice was loud and strong. You'd swear every word she said was true. She was someone you would want to be, someone that you would love. Oh, I wish I could walk across Africa with my sister, but now her jaw is frozen closed; the wind whistles through it like steam escaping. What she says are words of judgment, words of disgust, words of punishment. What she is holding down would come up clear and right. It is I *am*, down there. It is, I *do*, I *will*, I *can*. It is my sister, long lost.

Somewhere Else

Somewhere where we have boomerangs and we throw them out beyond the yard, over the roof of the house next door, above the trees, and they come back, right into our hands.

We play basketball with Dad (we have a dad) after dinner (we have dinner). Dad says, "Nice try." Dad says, "Great catch." Dad says, "Two points." Dad says, "Look at those muscles," and he puts his fingers on either side of our arms, says, "Wow."

Afterward, we all go raid the refrigerator. We take out milk and bread and pickles and mustard and bologna. There's plenty more where that came from. There are lines on the wall that show how we grow. We run back, jump on our very own beds until someone comes, combs our hair, tucks us in, says, "Nighty-night."

"Did you brush your teeth?" our mama says. We are not living at the shelter. Our mom is not working two jobs. We are not going into foster care for a few months until our mom can get a job that pays the rent.

Our mom has nothing better to do at night then to think about our teeth, our jammies, our storybook time.

I like vacation best. Mom and Dad take turns driving and navigating. We jump up and down, pull down our arms when a truck passes, look for signs with the right words and have to go to the bathroom. Then we get there and Dad says, "Go ahead," and we run down to the beach and into the water and the waves are big and the water just right. Mom and Dad think it's funny when I lift my shorts up so they won't get wet. At night we walk on the beach, Mom and Dad arm in arm and us finding shells. It is great, all of us together.

Nothing bad ever happens. Or, if it does, like if the dog makes a mess on the carpet or something, well, it can just be cleaned up. Nothing is ever an emergency.

I play baseball and when my turn comes up to bat it's quiet and the pitcher revs up and then the ball is in the air and I hear my dad whisper, "Let it go," and it's a bad pitch and then the pitcher revs up again and the ball comes just right and Dad says, "Hit it, hit it," and I swing the bat and smack, I hit it.

I run and run and all the way I hear Mom say, "Go, Kathy, go."

"Run, you can do it," Dad says, "go, go, go."

When it seems like first base is too far away and I am so slow (like dreams I have now) and the first baseman there is ready to make a catch with his toe on the base, I almost just stop, figure why even try, I'll never make it. Then I hear from behind the fence, from behind me, I hear, "Go. Run. Don't give up. You can make it. You can do it. Go. Go. Go."

I hear, "Go, go, go," and I do. I do. I slide in and I am safe and, oh, man, oh, man, it is great. It is the greatest.

Seventeen

We are not seeing ourselves here.

We are seeing ourselves in magazines with our jean buttons open, our hair long and straight. We are seeing ourselves looking up at the camera, lying back on steps that lead up to a building we are supposed to know about.

We are walking on cobblestones.

We are wearing geometry.

We are lying on our elbows with rippled hair that begins a rippled desert. We are on our tippy-toes, our knees; we are licking our fingers, popsicles. We need MOISTURE.

We are seventeen.

For now we are working at Sterry Rubber, at Burger King, at Sam's Steakhouse. For now we are needing a muffler, a box of Tide, to pay the hospital.

We are out on the stoop, thinking about the future, our future.

We are trying not to show.

Who we are are all women. We are all women in a warehouse room. We are wearing hairnets. We are wearing face masks. Covered in talc, we are a hundred, maybe more. Who we are are the inspectors. We are a roomful of inspectors. We are a roomful of inspectors under the fluorescent lights.

We are a room full of inspectors thump-pooshing our air buttons, blowing up our rubber gloves, looking for pinholes, defects. We are all women. We do not know why there are no men.

We are beginning to show.

Our water is supposed to break. We do not know what that means. Your water breaks, then you go to the hospital.

We are carrying trays of food through double doors. On one side everything is carpet, cool, candlelight, white tablecloths, red napkins, the clink of glasses, the muffled sound of ice shaking. On the other, everything is dropping, clanging, steel surface, slippery tile, plates of steak bones, steam, comfort, warmth.

All things are too much with us, our mothers say, too much of having to get and to spend. We are the girls that are beginning to show. Our mothers are at work. Our fathers we have not yet met. When the sun sets the boys will be snow under the streetlights, when the sun rises we will watch the fire hydrant water fall. We are the girls that you must see. We are on the outskirts of town, walking by the side of the road, standing in line. We are leaning on the porch with New York in our eyes, with Canton, Ohio, with Huntsville, Arkansas, San Pedro, Guatemala, Delhi there. We are the ones the men want to rock like a horse when we are a whir of dust, when we are too young. We are in the cane with no way out, in the warehouse room, back there under the bed, hiding.

We will take our diaper bags out. It is necessary for us to crawl across the railroad tracks, to hit the tops of our heads, to make a bigger graph, a longer curve. A hundred of us thump-pooshing our air buttons, with clouds above the fluorescent lights, with varicose veins to hide. Not for one moment are we not smiling, are we not polite, do we not commiserate.

Counting is not something that is done to us. We count the days until this, the hours until that. It is 11:49, 11:50, 3:24, 3:29, six months from a GED, almost closing time.

We are not seeing ourselves here. If we are walking by the side of the road, pushing a stroller, it is just because the bus was late. We cannot get one more pink slip. If you see us in line it is because we are thinking ahead, past the end of the line, way up front. We are seeing ourselves in the future, wearing something different than what we have on just now, in a place of our own.

We are not seeing ourselves here at the end of the line, explaining that our heat has been turned off, that we might need some help. We are not seeing ourselves being told that we make too much, but that if we do not get our heat back on by next week, she is sorry, but she will have to put our children in foster care.

We are still seeing ourselves in magazines. We want to be discussing date rape in a circle of girls from the dorm. We want to be discussing the health care system, giving input. We want to have our picture taken in front of our paintings. We want to take our shirts off in the park, to read our poetry up there at the mike.

Every page is something we want to see ourselves being. We are turning page after page, looking back and forth. There are boots and flannel, leather and dresses with flowers. What we are really looking for is ourselves. We are turning pages, looking at the background for a teething ring, a box of Pampers, a child running up behind with arms outstretched, hungry. We are not seeing teenagers who are mothers. There are no mothers at all. There are none of us who are part of the collective, setting up installations, chipping in for the lights, the set. It is not us there getting the tattoo, having something pierced, walking with the man with the baggy pants and the crew cut, living in the loft with the man who is also a sculptor, who is also in the band. We do not see any factory workers, no one with a hairnet on, a face mask. No one in a roomful of one hundred women thumppooshing our air buttons, trying to make quota. No one with an apron, a tray of drinks, no one in a hat from Burger King. No one like we are. We are still looking front to back. We have to be honest, to face up. We are not seeing ourselves here, not yet.

How I Became a Single Parent by Linda Vitale

So you don't get confused, here is a list of people who are going to pop up later on:

Tom—Debbie Russo's brother. Father of Marselina

Marselina—My first child

Dick—Father of my second child

Darrin—Possible father of Darrin

Harry—Father of my third child

Tracy—My third child

First, you probably want to make a joke about the father's names: Tom, Dick, and Harry, but I am asking you nicely, don't. Second, the background on this begins with my mother, a single parent, who, when my father left for good, broke every dish in the house, then chased him down the street for three blocks carrying the kitchen mirror that was over the bathtub and threw it in the middle of First Avenue when he jumped on a bus. Then she came home and put everything back together with my brother's airplane glue.

"That's one big mouth less to feed," my mother said.

The dishes ended up being a waste of glue because you had to eat your cereal fast to get any milk and because of the floor being sticky all the time.

Everyone complained about that.

My next topic, what we then called getting "knocked up," marked the beginning of me being an unwed mother. I'm fourteen and staying over at Debbie Russo's, drinking beer and watching *The Twilight Zone*, that one about when the earth gets out of control and heads toward the sun and everything plastic melts, including the radio, and then the earth misses the sun and everything gets cold and the melted things have icicles on them, when Debbie Russo's brother insisted I go back to his room to see his record player and he put on the Righteous Brothers' "You've Lost That Lovin' Feeling," and then he told me to take my clothes off and lay down on the floor. I said, "No way," and he said, "Only kidding," and then he did this Bill Cosby ice-cream routine and I did a Smothers Brothers' joke and then we made a tent over the bed and pretended we were in a spaceship. I got to be Flash Gordon and I let him be my copilot and we went to another galaxy where we lost the ability to talk and then we wrestled and tickled each other and then he pulled down my shorts and we did it, and then, after that, I was an unwed mother on account of the fact that Tom was too young to get his life messed up, everyone said.

I became a single parent about the time the garment factory moved to Brooklyn. All these hippies moved into the neighborhood and I met one, Dick, in Tompkins Square Park, and he said calling myself an unwed mother was uncool. Dick had long blond hair and wore suede fringe boots like an Indian and he took me to his place on First Avenue where the McDonald's is now and where he lived with other people who looked just like him. He showed me his corner where he had a mattress on the floor and Indian print cloths hanging all around and he lit a candle that had sand on it and gave me a rolled-up cigarette, which he said everybody smoked, and he said I should smoke it, too, because then I would be in solidarity with all the college students who were working for the good of all poor people everywhere. He called it a joint. Then he explained to me all about unconditional love, the collective unconscious, pacifism, Being Here Now, and then we did it.

I moved in right away. Morning had broken, we were stardust, we were golden, may the circle be forever and ever unbroken, we sang. We all sat in a big circle every night and became one. It was a new age, and I didn't want it ever to end. There were fifteen of us in the apartment, hundreds in the street. Dick said I was far out and we kissed with windowpane on our tongues. I felt while the earth moved somewhere under my feet.

I grew my bangs out, stopped putting eyeliner on, wore bell-bottoms, and carried Marselina in an army knapsack with holes cut in it for her legs.

"You look like a vagabond," my mother said to me after her work one day.

"Mama, the word is hippie. I look like a hippie."

"Like those vagabonds who eat out of the garbage and sleep on the street. Linda, that's what you look like."

"We have a generation gap, Mama," I said, "I can't talk to you now. It's normal."

"It's normal? A daughter throwing mud in her mother's face? A daughter who looks like a hipster?"

"Hippie, Mama," I said.

I had Darrin on a mattress in the middle of the floor and my new family all held hands in a circle around me. Darrin was our first child and we would have other children, children of the universe, who wouldn't be torn by strife and we would teach them well and feed them on our dreams.

First Dick went off with Renee, who was from France and wanted to go west across America. Just before he left, he said, "You and I are soul mates: spiritually, mentally, and physically. The whole kit and caboodle. We're like this," and he held up two fingers like they were cemented together, but I guess he meant it in a higher consciousness realm because I never saw him again. The others went off to India or back to college. I went back to Mama's on Ninth between B and C.

"What happened to the hippsies?" Mama said.

"They left, Mama."

"This neighborhood is like that other word you call yourself: a mother without a husband."

"Single parent, Mama."

"That's it. This neighborhood is like a single parent. Deserted."

Then the Japanese men bought the garment factory and things got hard at work because they didn't speak Italian and they raised the quotas.

"See what I mean?" Mama said, "The whole world is like a solitary mother."

"I don't get it, Mama."

"Linda, use your noggin," Mama said, putting two fingers against her temples and then out in the air like a bird's beak. "A mother alone has to fight, fight, fight all the time. That's what I mean." She poked me in the arm with the beak.

"Times have changed, Mama," I said.

"You're telling me something new?"

The way I got my third child shows just how much times had changed. Harry, who worked at the crack house on the corner, brought Tracy up one day and asked would I keep an eye on her for a couple of hours, and I said, "Okay, Harry, no problem. But that's two hours on the dot, no monkey business."

"I'll be back. You have my word," Harry said, and then he gave Tracy a kiss and kept standing at the door looking at her like it was killing him to leave, but something at the door was tugging him and then he came back and gave Tracy another kiss and he touched her face and then he put both his hands up in the air and said, "I'll be right back. Promise," and he made an X on his heart. Then he opened the door like he was afraid it would make noise and he tiptoed out into the hall and, as far as anybody knows, disappeared, completely disappeared, off the face of the earth.

He left a full box of Pampers.

Which, as I explained to Mama, is more than any of the other kids' fathers ever did give me.

Bonneville Salt Flats

The rest area: only thing growing is one blade of grass. Only thing moving is fake water at the end of the road, a fly in a barrel.

Nothing but pink dirt, pink cracked dirt.

"Jolene," my mom says, "Jolene, I ain't got but three cigarettes left."

I see things.

My mom smokes her cigarettes, one, two, three.

"Jeez," I say, "You see that? By the Men's?"

"Nothing there," my mom says, "I checked."

I keep my soap in a plastic dish, a rubber band around my toothbrush and toothpaste. I got a notebook, a pen, crayons, a brush, two shirts, an Etch A Sketch that doesn't erase no matter how much it's shook.

"Something moved," I say, "I swear."

"So check then," my mom says.

"You check," I say.

My mom used to give me baths in the sinks. Now I lean over and wash my own hair. If they got a faucet you got to hold down, my mom holds it down for me. "If we don't take care of each other, who will?" my mom says.

She's right. It's me and my mom and the road. I'm afraid my mom's going to get caught and then she'd go away for a long time, and then who would take care of her? Who would take care of me? We don't have any relatives. Alls we got is each other. I don't want my mom to get caught. I don't want anything bad to happen to her. I tell her she's got to stop, that revenge is bad karma. But she's on a mission, which I already told her a million times I don't agree with at all. She gets mad when I call her retro, but that's what she is: retro.

Retro. Retro. Retro.

"Jolene, go over there and see what's in that barrel. Maybe someone threw away a decent-sized cigarette. Maybe on the sidewalk, there."

How it is at night: on your left, you see stars. You turn on your right, you see stars. On your back, it's ping, ping, ping with the shooting ones. I sleep on my stomach, pull up the blanket.

Things I like best: Coke and gum.

I go in the Women's, check the trash. I hear it, a stall door in the Men's. Don't ever get trapped, my mom always says, but I am. I look up at the aluminum vent, at the door, wait, but don't hear a sound. I look in the metal boxes in the stalls. Nothing but Kotex, disposable diapers.

I hand over the butts. My mom is thin. She wears hip-huggers, a halter top, cork sandals. She's sitting on a suitcase. We see plenty with knapsacks and tents, but we got ourselves good Samsonite.

"Somebody is there," I say.

"Like I said, I checked," my mom says, "But I could be wrong."

What you would see from above: A huge circle of pink which is the Bonneville Salt Flats. A line straight across. In the middle, a rectangle (the restrooms), three marks (the picnic tables), two dots (us).

"We're not getting a ride," I say.

She rolls the butt between her fingers, lets the tobacco drop into her rolling paper, rolls it up, licks it, holds it between her fingers while she looks for her lighter.

"Shit," she says, "Jolene, you got any matches?"

"I saw it again," I say.

My mom's young.

"You look too young to have a child," people tell her.

"Some of us get lucky early," my mom says and kisses me on the top of my head.

"Never mind, I found it," my moms says. "Jolene, you remember Puerto Penasco? The stars?"

"My arm hurts," I say. I want the sleeping bag.

"Organ Pipe?" she says.

"Right here," I say, "way up inside the bone."

"Those jellyfish were a bummer, though. Jolene, I only borrowed the sleeping bag but once or twice."

"Are we going east or west?" I say.

My mom raises her shoulders, splays her hands. "I don't care," she says, "Whatever you want."

I'm twelve. I should be in sixth grade. I should be living in some ranch-style house, getting yelled at for messing up my room. I should be sprawled on some couch, eating potato chips and watching The Brady Bunch.

"I want some Fritos," I say.

"Shit, yeah," my moms says, "And onion dip and a Dr. Pepper. Strawberry shortcake. How about strawberry shortcake, Jolene?"

"I could go for a whole meal," I say.

"Me, too," my mom says.

There's not even any cars, not one.

How all this started: my mom read something in the paper about deadbeat dads and it made her mad.

"That was nasty, Jolene. Don't you start smoking, ever, you hear?"

"Yes, Ma'am," I say. I pick up the sleeping bag, dark yellow outside, lion and jungle flannel inside, unroll it on the picnic table.

"My arm," I say and hold it.

The last guy drove a Continental, built banks. The one before was a college professor. Before that a jeweler, a hitchhiker, a blackjack dealer, a transportation analyst, a foreman, an editor of children's books. They all say the same things. I try to warn them.

First it's blue sky, tan mountain, pink dirt. Then it's all pink. Then blue, orange, burnt sienna, then red and dark green, then midnight blue. Then the lights come on and it's all black. I turn on my back, get the Etch A Sketch, start making a maze on top of the other maze lines.

White spotlights are on us, just us.

I see him run around to the back of the Men's.
"Lookey here, Jolene. Look what I found," she says. She holds up a pack of cigarettes.
"Two," she says, "but one's broke."
She smokes them one, two, three.
"We got us one," my mom says.

"East," I say, "Not west." West is behind. Ahead is ahead.

I can't see what he's doing, but I see him, hunched over.

Where you might see us: on the on-ramp on the Samsonite. I have a sign that says El Paso or Chicago. When you get close, my mom stands up, puts her thumb up high, then higher, then even higher. You might drive on by but she doesn't look back. She keeps her eyes set on exactly the opposite direction of where she wants to get. Me, my eyes are peeled straight ahead, past everything that is in my way, past the rushing and passing and veering for a spot, past the signs with arrows pointing off to the side, past where the road gets wavy and watery, past where it completely disappears, but who's paying attention to me.

You start in the middle of the Etch A Sketch, write "END," then make the maze lines around it.

What they all say: Yeah, they do have kids. Super-smart kids. Silas gets straight As. Shawn is a dancer. Brian can read twenty pages a minute. Mara's way advanced for her age. Why here's a picture of Nina. She's an angel. The cutest thing. Melissa loves her Daddy; why last time he saw her she clung to his leg like this, didn't want no part of going back. He's just so proud. Jesse plays on the hockey team. He's just like his dad. They are all just like their dad.

What they all say next: No, he's real lucky that way. The mothers take care of everything. The mothers have good jobs. They have their own life. They are busy with night school. They work for the city. They work doing nails. They work two jobs, get food stamps to boot. They got a scholarship. He's off the hook.

The thing in the newspaper made my mom mad. My mom says she's got to talk some sense into these dads, make them see the error of their ways. I tell my mom she's retro, all wrong. That all of this is like a tidal wave, no stopping it, no going backward. I read. I know things, too. Wish I could be at the library right now, matter of fact.

"Hiya, ladies," he says. He's jumping like ants in the pants, like a shaked-up Coke, a just runned over rat. Flyaway hair. Jeans too big.

I should be whining about having to do the dishes. I should be driving adults batty with my violin. Someone's supposed to tell me to do my homework. I'm supposed to still want stuffed animals, be worried about my period starting.

"Oh, you scared me," my mom says. "Where'd you come from? Weren't nobody here but ten minutes ago."

"From outer space. Just come down to protect you ladies. Crash landed."

"Protect yourself. Shut up and protect yourself," I say. I always warn them. I'm innocent.

"Jolene," my mom says.

"Have no fear, Frankie's here. Just here to protect you ladies," he says. He holds up his knife, the kind you can buy at Stuckey's.

"You got a cigarette?" my mom says.

He holds up Marlboros.

"Jolene," my mom says, "Would you mind getting me one of Frankie's cigarettes and a light?"

I go over, take one, wait while he checks his pockets for a light. I wish there weren't so many. I am tired of the Etch A Sketch.

"I want another Judy Blume book," I say. I got the last one from the editor. Didn't even put up a fight.

"I want some ESPRIT clothes," I say.

"Don't start now, Jolene," my mom says.

Once I ran away, but I couldn't get a ride.

"Look, anything goes wrong, Frankie'll take care of it. I'm Mr. Fix-it. Mr. Whatever-you-want. I'm Mr. Answer-to-your-prayers."

He goes on and on like that, taking his knife out, giving my mom cigarettes, telling her how she's all alone, no one to take care of her, how it sure was good he happened along when he did.

"Sure is," my mom says. Why she was plumb out of cigarettes, she says. Frankie is heaven-sent, a gift from God.

"Jolene sure is a looker," he says. "You two sisters?"

"Jeez," I say. I put down the Etch A Sketch, pull up the covers, turn over, listen for the road.

"Oh, Frankie. She's not my sister. Why, she's my daughter."

"No," Frankie says.

"It's the God-forsaken truth," my mom says. "You got any kids, Frankie?"

And he does. One in Florida, three in Ohio, one in Massachusetts. Beautiful, look just like him. Smart, too. He's got pictures.

"Must keep you pretty busy supporting all those kids, Frankie."

"No, not really," he says. He's got it made. No problem. Two of the mothers live with their own mothers. The other one won't answer the phone. Everything is taken care of.

"Is that right?" my mom says.

That's right. Same old stuff, like I already mentioned.

I close my ears. I used to worry maybe something would go wrong. But now I don't. Not with my mom.

Next morning we get a ride before eight.

"Jolene," my mom says, "I got to quit smoking, but I'm afraid to try. I'd hate to find out I can't."

"He was a jerk," I say, "A real jerk."

"I slept like a log. How about you, Jolene?"

What my mom does: ties them up. Takes all their money, then sends it to the moms.

What I want to do: live in a big house. Have a bike. Have my own room and just watch TV all day. Maybe even get on the Internet. Maybe I want to have a desk. Maybe I want to make a cartoon book. Maybe I want to go around, see what other people do.

"Now how we ever going to afford a house, Jolene?" my mom says.

"We can live with other moms and kids. We could all share. Honest, Mom, it'd be lots better than this."

"That's an idea, Jolene. That's an idea."

"I'm tired of this," I say. "I hope we never see one more dad."

"I'll tell you what, Jolene. I'll quit on the spot if the next five we ask, we got to let go." She means if they aren't dads, or if they pay child support, or if they're married, joint custody, that kind of thing.

"Great," I say as we head into Reno.

Reno, all alone there at the end of the road, pushing its way out of nothing. It looks just like the kind of place, all lit up before noon, all action, all quick, quick, quick, where things could come out good, where people like us, that never have any, could find some luck.

Revelations

Somewhere between the car lot in Smyrna, Arkansas, where Dottie bought her new used car, and the Sonic Drive-In in Sardis, Dottie had her vision. The one that told her to build Heaven and Earth. "Make it big, loud and smelly," she heard. She saw every detail, all the way down to using the Ban roll-on deodorant balls for the eyes. Even before she had the full truckload of sand dumped on top of the narcissus and iris bed, which made Margaret Kerr take down with sick headaches, since it'd been her dead husband who planted all those bulbs, all of Sardis knew that Dottie was up to something because a Xeroxed flyer was in all the mailboxes.

"Dear Friends," it said, "I'm working on a big project and need your junk. Please put all trash that isn't mushy garbage in cardboard boxes and set out by the road. I'll be around Mondays and Thursdays to collect. Thanks, Dottie Barr."

It wasn't Dottie's first vision. That happened when she was ten. Everyone else at church camp was singing, "You Can't Get to Heaven in a Limousine," and Dottie was bored, rubbing her eyes to get those great color designs, when BAM, two graham crackers appeared with marshmallows and Hershey's chocolate melting in between. Later, around the campfire, there they were: s'mores. "God's put me on this earth for something really big," Dottie thought.

She grew up, having many visions. Most were common, like seeing the face of the person whose phone call she was about to pick up, or seeing the naughty dachshund Aunt Polly would bring on her visit. Others were more helpful, like seeing the answers on tests, or seeing the final picture before she would begin painting. Sometimes she would go for years without any signs. After high school, Dottie, like most girls in Sardis, got married, had a child, then got divorced. Then she got a scholarship to Pratt and she and her daughter, Alma, went north for four years. One night on the beach in Southampton, where she went with some other Pratt students, Dottie had her greatest vision. Maybe it was just the stars. Maybe it was the boy from Queens she had fallen in love with. Dottie saw the stars and the ocean and her daughter and just about everything, even Aunt Polly's dachshund, as though it was all one big s'more, all squashed together. Even though she'd been saved back in Sardis by a traveling evangelist that played the electric guitar, Dottie knew her life was going to be both very hard and very easy after that moment.

Dottie came back to Sardis and got a job designing publications at a college in the next town. Then she bought the Kerr place, which was a good deal: a shotgun house in the middle of all the mansions on Murray Hill. Dottie and Alma were then what you might call set up, in the modern sense of the word. But it must have been too much for her, or maybe not enough. Dottie was relieved when she finally had, coming back from Smyrna in her new used car, the vision that would tell her not what was about to be, or what is, but what she should do. Life was going to be as straight and as smooth as the blacktop highway that points north from Smyrna to Sardis.

First thing she did after the vision was cut all the branches off her trees and stick jars on the ends. That took care of the obstructions. Then she piled tires on top of each other into a Roman-looking arch right where her front walk left the sidewalk. Next, she rented a lighted sign which sat on its trailer on the curb and flashed yellow arrows toward the yard. H E A V E N A N D E A R T H, it said. Then Dottie went right on working a forty-hour week and spending the rest of her time welding and cementing Heaven and Earth together.

At the end of her straight walk and in front of her porch, she welded iron bedsprings together into a huge chair shape, which she covered with aluminum foil. A naked Ken doll with pink Daisy razors superglued in its mouth sat in the middle. On each side, twelve hickory fence posts stood guard, all with heads. A cow's skull. An orange plastic pumpkin. A Prince Albert can with a variegated wig. Twenty-four in all. On one side some spelled out Heaven, on the other, Earth.

On the Earth side a huge lamb with rusty Brillo pads for fur and seven Ban roll-on deodorant balls for eyes jerked its head back and forth like a puppy with a shoe in its mouth. Seven lit-up Christmas angels marched across the roof, which Dottie painted with black and white stripes. Dottie went to Tulsa and brought back a huge blinking disco floor, which, turned up on its side, made the body of the red dragon on the Heaven side. Seven heads, made out of rusty wringer washers with rearview mirrors for eyes moved back and forth. Bicycle chains clanged inside.

Lawn sprinklers snaked along between whirligigs and made rainbows in the sunlight. If you walked by and stepped in the right place on the sidewalk, a hundred xylophones along the white picket fence pinged as you walked along. The angels on the roof blinked on and off and made a little jump after each blink. A burning vat of roofing rubber smoked and stank under the red dragon. A satellite dish rotated and broadcast the sound of aphids sucking on marigold stems below.

Heaven and Earth was a swarming, steaming, stinking mass of art.

Alma was ten when Dottie started making Heaven and Earth. Before that Dottie and Alma used to somersault down Murray Hill. Do cartwheels in the front yard. Swim in the river. Ride around in Dottie's convertible or walk arm in arm down the street. When Dottie started making Heaven and Earth, Alma began to wander in Sardis alone. The other kids at school would tease her: "Your mama's crazy. Your mama's crazy," they'd chant. Alma hated Dottie, Heaven and Earth, and Sardis.

Then Alma took up with the town rowdies and dropped out of high school. She'd wear tight jeans and Harley Davidson T-shirts frayed just below her bra. Dottie would be working with an acetylene torch on Heaven and Earth in overalls and construction boots, while Alma and her friends would be inside blaring heavy metal music.

"That's all you care about is that junk in the front yard," Alma would scream at Dottie.

"I care about you," Dottie would yell back.

"I wish Heaven and Earth had never happened," Alma thought. One night Alma decided to destroy Heaven and Earth, once and for all.

Alma and her friends pulled up with four flatbed trucks from one of her friend's dad's construction company and all of Sardis went quiet when they unplugged Heaven and Earth. They'd got the blinking sign, the tire arch, and were almost to the throne when Dottie came home. Dottie just stood there watching. Then she put the grocery bags down and just slumped down right there under the place where the arch used to be.

"Alma," one of the kids said, "This is your mom's art. Maybe we should put it back." The rest seemed to agree. The peer pressure was too great and Alma relented. Alma went off with her friends, though, and Dottie couldn't get her to come back.

A much improved Heaven and Earth was back together, clanging and blinking and stinking in no time. Dottie's neighbors started a court order to stop Heaven and Earth and were going around town getting support. Margaret Kerr told everyone it was the work of the devil. Kay Craftwright complained about the noise and the roofing tar smoke, which blackened the whole side of her house. Mark Cunningham told everyone that the roofing tar smoke got up in your lungs, attacked the sex parts of all your cells, and caused cancer. Others complained about the razor blades stuck in the tire arch. So, it seemed, all of Sardis was united against Heaven and Earth for a while, but by the next year it had brought the movie people, so Sardis was split right down the middle.

They weren't really movie people. They were music video people who came in the fall and almost corrupted Sardis. First the photographer from Little Rock came and took a picture of Heaven and Earth for the *Arkansas Gazette*.

Then the magazine people came. Then quicker than the gnats come up at dusk, Sardis was swarming with movie people and musicians who came to make a music video right in Heaven and Earth. They filled up the Shangri-La motel and Oleo Acres Campground. Everywhere they went, they left a big pile of money.

Bought six truckloads of sand and dumped it on Dottie's street to make it look like a dirt road. Then paid the Drake boys to clean it up. Had Doyle Knox bring his barbecue pit out to Oleo Acres and cook a pig for one of their parties. They bought everything in town and didn't even haggle about prices. Almost everyone had a part as an extra, which meant you stood around in a costume and were supposed to be one of the multitudes around Heaven and Earth. It was the first time most of Sardis had ever got paid with a check, not to mention being on TV.

When they started shooting, Dottie went to New York to see about a commission to make a sculpture. Alma took up with the movie people, stopped hanging around with the town rowdies, and moved back into the house. She started dressing arty like the movie people and just whizzed about right there in the center of the action, running errands and holding lights. She even got the best spot as an extra. She was the only real angel of the seven angels on the roof and she played a trumpet in the first shot. One night after the movie people had all gone back to their trailers, Alma sat in the middle of Heaven and Earth and had her first vision.

She looked at the whirligigs and remembered when Dottie taught her to do cartwheels. She looked at the lamb and remembered when her mother held her and they cried together because their puppy had been hit by a car. She looked at the sprinkler and remembered running through it into Dottie's arms. She heard the bicycle chains clang inside the wringer washers of the dragon and she felt her mother's anger, heard her yelling at her. She looked at the cement mixer and the acetylene torch and felt her mother desert her.

"I want, I want, I want, I want," Alma said out loud. "I want, I want, I want, I want, I want, I want," she said over and over, louder and louder. Then Alma noticed that branches were growing out of the underside of the bottled limbs of the trees and it had leaves again. She saw that the wisteria vine was crawling up the side of the house and overtaking the last milky white angel on the roof. She saw that the burning vat of tar was gone. She saw that honeysuckle was growing over the fence and covering the tire arch and the xylophones. She saw the stars. "Heaven and Earth isn't everything," she said to herself, "and neither is my mother," and she got up and went in the house to make plans.

Before Dottie came back from New York, Alma moved to the trailers with the movie people. "This world is really something," Alma thought when they offered her a job as an assistant's assistant and asked her to come back to Hollywood with them. But just when they were almost finished, when they had only one more week of shooting to go, the anti–Heaven and Earth faction in Sardis got a court order to destroy it. The shopkeepers and others making money off the movie people had tried everything to stop the court order, but in the end they lost. Electricians had gone out and disconnected Heaven and Earth and two bulldozers were parked facing each other on the sidewalk in front of it the night Dottie came back. She read the condemned notice on the front fence.

"At 8:00 tomorrow morning Heaven and Earth will be gone," Dottie read. She went in the house, got a quilt and pillow, and settled into the scoop of the bulldozer on the Heaven side of Heaven and Earth. "Nothing lasts forever," she said and she closed her eyes hoping for a vision of the next sculpture she would do. When she opened them Alma was walking up the street towards her.

"Hi," Alma said. Then she marched across in front of Dottie and settled into the scoop of the other bulldozer. Dottie threw Alma a blanket. "I'll miss the lamb most of all," Alma said.

"Really?" Dottie said, "I always liked the dragon best."

"What are you going to do? Are you going to get out of the scoop when they start the bulldozers?"

"Of course," Dottie said, "but I thought I'd protest some first."

"Me, too," Alma said.

So Heaven and Earth was destroyed and eventually Sardis came to miss it, or at least the tourist money it might have brought. Alma went off to Hollywood and eventually to Cal Arts to study film and still works there now, happy as can be to be in the middle of a production. Dottie went to New York, then Chicago to make sculpture. After a while, she moved to Pasadena, where she welcomes Alma's children every Saturday to come and make cookies, to make wild art projects, to run through sprinklers, to go to museums, and to do cartwheels and somersaults. She is Grandma Dottie in her overalls and construction boots. She sold the shotgun house on Murray Hill to an accountant who planted zoysia grass in the yard and created the flattest, greenest, lushest, and most boring yard Sardis had ever seen.

Yonder's Wall

For Randy Feemster, Dean Root, Skip Brick, and Lavelle Evans

First week back, Sam's at the taxidermist.

"How'd you lose it?" the taxidermist asks while he's measuring.

"Pongee stick," Sam says.

Sam puts the prosthetic devices and the cow stump and the horse stump on the table. The cow leg he had gotten from some Mennonites out by Navarre. The horse leg had been the leg of Yonder's Wall, a Kentucky Derby–bound thoroughbred who himself had met with an unfortunate leg accident and had to be shot.

"Can you put them together? Make me a leg for work, a leg for show?" Sam says.

The taxidermist nods, picks up the horse leg and starts to work.

"Why can't you wear one of those nice flesh-colored legs like everyone else?" Sam's mother says, when Sam finally goes home, "Or a wooden one?"

Sam wants to make up for lost years. In Nam, radios had blared about being experienced, counting to four and asking what it is we were fighting for, and Sam sees himself on the road with half a million strong heading for a new Woodstock, even better than the one he'd missed. He wants to be a part of that great mass of students who protested, put flowers in their hair, hitchhiked across America, made love to everyone, and talked about touching souls, higher consciousness, and out-of-body experiences.

"I want to have an out-of-body experience," he says at a bar one night.

"A what?" someone asks.

"An out-of-body experience. Astral projection. You know, a spiritual trip," Sam says.

The heads shake no, stare ahead.

"That's nice, Sam," someone says.

Sam uses the GI Bill and signs up for classes: World Civilization, English, American Society, Art. The students snicker about growing marijuana in their dorm rooms and brag about getting falling-down drunk on a Saturday night. Sam tries to join their discussions, but they stop talking and stare at him as though he's a narc or the president of Dow Chemical, or, even worse, a veteran of the Vietnam War. Once, after practicing in the mirror for several weeks and bumbling several attempts, he finally asks one of them out on a date.

"No one dates anymore," she says. Then she walks off, flicking her long blond hair behind her.

Hobbling on the cow's foot in the sculpture room, Sam grows his black beard and hair long and wears overalls without a shirt, exposing a wide, hairy chest and a long, ugly scar on his right arm beside which is tattooed: Da Nang 1/6/69. The instructors, accustomed to seeing abstract or psychedelic paintings or shapes carved out of wood or made of plaster, ignore Sam's work, which has troughs of growing rice, mazes of straw peppered with bullets, Polaroid photos of Vietnam, and 4' x 10" blocks of steel on which he painted faces of buddies he'd known.

"No one paints portraits anymore," the instructors finally say to him.

"No one?" Sam asks.

"No one. Study art history," they say, "Art is not real life. It's the arrangement of color and shape on a two-dimensional surface in the case of painting, or in space in the case of sculpture."

"That's all?" Sam asks.

"Either that or visual puns," they say and flunk him.

The campus's chapter of Vietnam Veterans Against the War is going to Washington DC for a demonstration. Sam goes back to his mother's house to get the Purple Heart he was given for losing his leg. He searches though the can openers, broken spatulas, corks, pennies, buttons, and pieces of string in the bottom of the kitchen drawer until he finds it. In Washington, Sam throws the medal into the chicken-wire enclosure where it burns with the others, but, since no one is there but a handful of senior citizens who apparently got separated from their tour, it isn't as satisfying as Sam hoped it would be.

He limps off to a street vendor and buys three hot dogs, spilling mustard down the front of his overalls.

"This is the end of my political career," Sam says to the vendor.

"It's not like it used to be. No more sit-ins, love-ins, moratoriums. Business has gone all to hell."

"But what am I going to do now?" Sam piles relish on his fourth hot dog.

"What can you do?" the vendor looks at the cow leg.

"Get bit by mosquitoes. Sit around and wait. Be angry."

"Not much call for that," the vendor says, "How about when you were younger? What could you do then?"

"Play pool," Sam says, brightening.

In the beginning Sam plays pool. Six hours a day. Then he shoots. Bank shots. Around the world. Kiss, massé, and carom shots. Two, four, and six ball combinations. He can sink the eight ball on a break. He can use English to make the cue ball hit a ball in a side pocket, go downtown to tap a ball into a far pocket, hit a bank where it picks up speed and cuts a ball into a pocket uptown. Then the cue ball comes to rest softly in front of the eight ball for an easy win. Sam takes off Yonder's Wall's leg and lays it on the side of the pool table for long shots. He lives above the pool hall and sometimes sleeps on the steps halfway up to his room, not making it all the way every night.

"Is that alive?" a woman says at the bar one night, "I mean is it real?" She lifts up Sam's pant leg and touches the fur on the horse leg.

"Wild," she says.

"Wild?" Sam says, "Wild? No, this horse was not wild. It was domesticated."

"But you're wild, right?" the woman says, her foot slipping on the bar stool, her head bobbing in Sam's direction.

"Yes," Sam says, "I am." That night he decides he can't go back up to his room, and he walks out of the bar and out in the street, where he keeps walking for the next few years.

"I can make my own observations and draw my own conclusions," Sam says. Sam looks everywhere in every city he can.

"What are you looking for?" a homeless man asks him one day. Sam shrugs.

"Are you looking for the lunch ladies? The lunch ladies is over there, through that door." He motions to a door under a Catholic Worker Lunch Program sign.

"Go on," the homeless man says, "That's what you're looking for. They're nice. They got everything right there. Honest."

And that's where Sam stays, there in that town, at that place. He washes the dishes. He wears the cow leg. Puts snow seal on the hoof to keep it clean and dry. On his good leg he wears a rubber boot. The dishes pile up. He scrapes them, rinses them, and stacks them into bins. He lifts the sides of the dishwasher, slides in a rack and pushes out a clean one on the other side. Then he pulls out the dishes and stacks them on a shelf behind him. By the time he turns back the counter is full of dirty dishes. He circles, circles, circles on the cow's leg, the hoof stuck in the mesh mat.

It is the thing that is missing, the thing that cannot be seen, what is absent, empty; this is the thing that roots him, that is most full, that is strongest, that is most present.

Journal Found in a Field

There is here so much work and it is only us four. We have rags, which are clean, alcohol for sterilizing, and adhesive tape. Marcy went out and gathered enough straight wood for splints, but as of yet we can't use them. The wagon, for which we are thankful, still has its wheels.

Yesterday we came over the hill and saw it for the first time. The entire valley all luminous red, moving ever so slightly. A finger twitching, a body rolling over, an arm reaching up. It was not that we could, say, look out over the field and choose one most in need. No, we started at our feet and treated each person in the order we came upon them. Devon and Max pulled out the stretchers but quickly recognized the absurdity of that. We had no reason to move anyone anywhere.

I opened the packages of rags, breaking the sterile tape and Marcy, with her gloves on, picked up a wad and stuffed them in the worst holes.

"Bless you," they said.

"Thank you," they said. Those that could talk.

Where we got the supplies: when they closed the hospitals years ago, Devon and I broke in, saving what we could carry away in the van. We even got the autoclave, which, old as it is, is the most important piece of equipment we had. Before we set out, we used it to sterilize everything we could use as a bandage. The EKG machine, the sonogram, etc., have been, as you can imagine, of no use. Besides, they are back at the house. At first, if someone was missing a limb, we looked for it to try to keep limb and body together but we soon abandoned that futile effort. Here again, the sterile rags, alcohol, and adhesive tape are our best tools. We press, stuff, bind, and tie off.

Pouring the alcohol is the worst part, but Marcy thinks it gives us a good indication as to their ability to react and the depth of the shock. Those that scream and try to move away are our most hopeful prospects for recovery. We had thought we would see helicopters or ambulances but we have had no sign of life outside. We have begun to wonder if news is getting out of the country. Surely someone out there will object, will come to our aid.

Marcy wants to go back to the house to see if our radio works, but we can't spare her just yet. Our consensus was to get to each casualty first, to give a rag, a drink of water, some comfort to everyone, then to go back to the house together as a group.

I was holding a head, a hand, while Devon stuffed a stomach, when we saw them up over the hill in a line in their blues and browns, well-shaven, their artillery gleaming. The horses, the horses, steaming and stomping and the tanks like turtles. Box turtles. Then, behind that, came the others with their digital film cameras, riding in those sport-utility vehicles that have become so popular with them now. Max said he saw their Leader, the one that used to be the brunt of so many cartoons and comedians, lurching down the hill followed by people Max guessed must be making a movie.

"What could he be doing?" I asked Max.

"It seems like he is trying to get a better look," he said. But then their Leader came close enough that I could see, too. He put a foot up on one of the bodies on the edge, raised his arm in a muscle man or Heisman trophy–type pose and looked into the camera.

"It's an interview," Max said.

I had the head in my lap. I gently moved it back to the ground and curled around it. I saw Marcy and Devon also get low. We were bloodied enough by now to blend in, to be camouflaged.

The woman with the hatchet still in her back said that maybe they were just admiring their work, and yes, it did seem to be the case. They streamed out of their cars and positioned themselves on the field. It looked like they were going to start a fire; someone was lifting bags of charcoal from the trunk of a car. Others set up tables, chairs, unfurled red-and-white checked tablecloths. There were six-packs and liter bottles of Coke and McDonald's for the kids, all of which made us conclude that they hadn't killed every one of us, that there were still workers in the world alive. It was those bags that changed our plans.

Three days pass and we lay there in our own shit and piss and the smell of the field with our own dead.

There is nowhere now, we decide, where they are not and we begin to regret that we had not been at the battle, that we did not fight, even though we are pacifists and cannot. Still, those on the hill had such an air of complete victory that when we saw them we began to wish we were not able-bodied since we found ourselves beginning to fill up with such desire for revenge, for violence. We almost began to envy the dead and even the wounded, especially those who seem to have lost all feeling, since they seem so at peace. At least they are free of hope.

At night, we inch along the ground to continue our work, taking water, rags, and alcohol, though we use alcohol sparingly since we are afraid of screams, which would be so out of the ordinary sounds of moans and calls for help here. Then by day we sleep.

They are still here.

Surely there is somewhere for them to go back to. Surely they can return to their homes, those homes we used to laughingly call McMansions. We assume they have taken over everywhere, even back at our house.

Still, we are four able-bodied and we have been finding more like the woman with the hatchet in her back who are not so hurt, and she, the hatchet now removed, the wound cleaned and covered, has started to assist. Another man who appears to have only lost an ear (for what?) has joined our ranks. As we go over the field we hope to find more. When the sun comes up we lie together, wondering. We know now we are in the safest place imaginable, here in the ranks of the wounded, of our own, though Devon said some went over to the other side early and now act as infiltrators, ready to begin the resistance from within. The rest of us said we doubted it, that those who went over went for money, for their own greed and are now lost to us forever.

The plan now, after seeing the McDonald's bags, is to continue as we are until one of us has a chance to get back to the house, look and see the condition, then report back to us. Marcy has volunteered.

My bed. My bed.
I hope no one is sleeping in my bed.

What the McDonald's bags mean to us: that there are others of us out there, that there are still workers in the world.
"Where there are workers, there is a chance to organize," Max says. "There is a chance to unite, take over."
Oh, hope. It will be the death of me.

Luckily it has not rained but there is a ring around the moon tonight. My back hurts. I want some food: bread, butter, a meal. We have what we are calling the biscuits, which are sustaining us. We are feeding those that cannot feed themselves.
What the biscuits really are: Ol' Roy dog food. It is food from the bowels of the enemy, from their Wal-Mart, but we are eating it. Devon had found the bags in an old abandoned storage unit and brought them to us before, before this, what we can only call the final massacre. We have four bags left.
We are growing in numbers.
We are now fourteen.

We have debates at night. A plan of escape? Or a plan of attack? We four always vote for escape, noting that we do not yet know what is beyond, but those whose numbers are growing are wanting revenge. "Let us find life," we say. "We have not yet covered the field. They finally agree. We may have to leave the field, to leave those so in need," we say, "but only in hopes of returning with real help." They nod, agree through their bandages.

"After all," Devon says, "we saved your life."

"So now we have to go along with whatever you say? We have to sit here mamby pampy helping when we could be taking their fucking cameras and stuffing them down or up their orifices?"

Who can blame them for their anger? Those from the hill now traipse over here, stepping over bodies and pointing their cameras down on the worst of those injured. When someone jiggles or has spasms or yells out they all run over as one body. Some have sticks they use to see if there is life, if they can stir up movement. Then at night they use the footage, showing it between the movies they watch. We can see their big plasma screen from here.

We decide to move tonight, but vote that Marcy should not go alone. Half of us will go, half stay. The more able-bodied, us four, and a few others will slide on our stomachs out to the woods. Then we will crawl on all fours to the house.

To the occupied house, I should say. I cried and held myself still. They were definitely in my bed. We then set out for the closest neighbor, but that is also occupied. It is then that we decide on attack, we pacifists, but we must go back and confer, to inform our cohorts.

We roll into the field. Roll, stop, roll, stop. Our movement cannot be noticed. The grass is thick and tall.

The hatchet woman has died, blood is still flowing out of her mouth. But there are now twenty-three of us and we are divided almost in half. Ten will form the "army." I myself say no, yes, no, yes, no, yes, no, yes. To go against my principles so late in my life you would think was ludicrous, but I ask you, would you not feel as though you'd missed everything if you did not go?

You see how wrong begets wrong.

We first devise our weapons, our plan of attack, our positions, all the while continuing our work. Max, who is on the side wanting to stay, points out that if we have rain, they may end their picnic and go on. Then we could stay, he asserts, and increase

our ranks as more are healed. But by now, everyone is so sickened
by the drunken antics from the hill that the war cry is practically
a consensus. Even Max seems to be wavering. We present our
case to the others. After much argument we have devised a plan
without violence, but with much drama and artifice. Our hope is
to entice their Leader, along with his cameras, down to the field
where some of us will stage a fight, as though the wounded had
turned against themselves. I will have the hatchet, a bayonet to
flail around and, then, at a moment such as the one at the end
of Hamlet, when all appear dead, we will rise up and take their
Leader as our (and this is the part we pacifists are still objecting
to) hostage. It is I who will express, eloquently, I hope, our list of
demands into the cameras.

I feel such fear, such excitement even saying the words to the
others.

Max points out a problem with our plan, that we, in our
enthusiasm, (or is it hunger?) have overlooked. Hostage-takers,
he points out, have to have some place to hide their hostages,
some place that is secret; secrecy is the power of hostage-takers,
and we, exposed as we are in the field, have none. Of course, we
can see the truth in what he says and then, of course, we all say,
we were not truly, in our hearts, behind the scheme. Max begins
what will assuredly be a speech to match Lincoln's or Kennedy's
or Dr. Martin Luther King's in its importance to history, a speech
in which he points to the McDonald's bags and other proof that
somewhere in the world are more of us, that we will make it out to
join the others, that we will use all of our riches, all of our talents,
all we have to offer, and we will, we will succeed.

It is been decided that after we have reached everyone in the
field, we will leave all but the medical supplies and the remaining
dog biscuits (I will have to leave my precious book and pen) and,
quiet as lambs, we will slither out on our bellies and continue our
work. "Long live the pacifists," Max whispers and we join him,
on down the line, repeating the words over and over. And in areas

of the field that we have not yet been able to reach, we hear more whispers that join ours." Long live the pacifists. Long live the pacifists. Long live the pacifists," we sing all night long, united now and ready.

My Lot

I am down on my knees, digging.

It is my lot. I work on one square foot a day, pulling out broken bottles, rocks, needles, works, dead roots, crack vials, little tiny plastic Ziploc bags, weeds, rusted nails, screws, bolts.

The three children who live in the apartment building come to help me. Together we get down on our knees. "Little by little," I say, "is how we make a garden."

"Little by little," the children say over and over, chasing each other around and around the lot. We dig up the dirt and break up the clumps. The children take the grass seed from the bag and throw it on our little square. We smooth the earth with the palms of our hands and water it with a bucket. Sometimes their father sits in the chair beside the building and watches us. He is up and down the steps all night, out for crack, in to smoke, out for crack, in to smoke, out for crack and so on. Eyes as big as Manga, arms as thin as a brownish glass pipe, you'd think he was weak, but he can break apart a door, hurl himself against a wall, jump up high enough to catch hold of a fire escape, swing himself up or walk all night looking down at the curb. Upstairs I hear furniture being thrown, glass being broken, thuds and stomps.

We gather up our tools to go inside. We put the little spade, the fork, the gloves in a box. When I pass their father, I nod, say hello.

"You won't get anything to grow here," he says.

I am a Mennonite. We are allowed four professions: farmer, peace worker, teacher, or social worker. This world, the Mennonites say, is not the real world.

When she was invited, my mother used to go next door to hear music. The neighbor knew we had no music in our house. I would sneak in the space between our houses and stand under the window to listen. When my mother came home she sat on the couch and looked up in the air. "I saw blue," she said, "blue floating through the air."

Recently I got down on my knees and asked my mother to forgive me. I started with little things I had done, fighting with my brother, for example, breaking a window. Then I added bigger things which would make the Seven Deadlies or the Ten Commandments seem superficial and quaint. Most of the bad things involved ways to get the part of her that lived in me to die. Though she's been dead for ten years she still comes to talk to me and sometimes touch me, even though she never touched me when she was alive. She lifted me once when I was running down a hill, spoke to me while I was swimming in a pool in the Bronx. She told me she was sorry, that she was trying to beat my alcoholic father out of me. I told her I understood. I have tendencies.

The lot had been lined by the ailanthus trees that make life worth living in New York City. They just up and died one day, all of them, like they had been poisoned. That is why I was able to put in the garden. Suddenly sunlight hit the ground. From my window on the third floor I watched the father pull the gray, bare trunks down with a rope, jumping out of the way at the last minute as they fell. Then he lifted the trunks onto a broken chair and cut them up with a rusty saw. He will do anything for five dollars.

Other dead come to me, not just my mother. Sometimes that is how I know they died. Once I dreamed that an old lover of mine and I were riding on a roller coaster. It clanged to the top of the hill, then when it jolted ahead and the front part was headed down and our little roller-coaster car was at the top, he stood up and jumped. I looked over the edge and saw his body down below, tiny and splayed out, a crowd gathering. Then in a dream in a dream, he came to me after he died.

"Why did you jump?" I asked. "I would have loved you."

But he looked at me, saw right through me, didn't believe a word and, of course, he was right; I was incapable of such a love as that. A drummer I knew in Arizona, a Vietnam veteran who once told me I could reconfigure, came to talk to me, too, while

I sat on the floor in New York and that's how I knew he was dead and it was true, he had died at that very moment.

I am not a good Mennonite. My brother is better. He lives the simple life in Pennsylvania. He appears to have no ambition, no expectations, no vision of himself as anyone more than someone who stacks oranges in a grocery store. There appears to be no wrestling match between two internal cartoon characters; one saying "I want, I want, I want, I can, I will," and the other with a hand grasping the neck of the first, throwing it to the ground, pinning it with the words of "Just try it, buddy. Just try it." The dead come and talk to my brother, too. He told me that after my mother died, as he was driving, he felt her presence huge over his left shoulder, and there she was in a hearse, speeding along to the funeral home.

The drummer grew gourds in gardens hidden in the Arizona canyons. He would cut the gourds, then paint them, stain them, and sell them. He wandered in the desert, never talking to anyone, but he talked to me. At night he would meditate sometimes until dawn. He told me he was from Bed-Stuy. "I killed people," he said, "And not just one or two."

The kids kneel down with me. We dig up one square foot a day. We are digging holes then putting in impatiens: white, rose, and red. We place rocks carefully around the flowers. "Which one is right for here?" I ask.

"This one," the littlest girl says. She is three with big brown eyes and straight black hair in pigtails that stick out. We make a winding walkway through the grass, choosing the flattest rocks.

"Little by little," we say and we put in narcissus, marigolds, horseradish, nettles, iris, aster, lady's slipper, and morning glories that climb up the twenty-foot high fence that separates the lot from the schoolyard. The powder-blue morning glory flowers are cushioned in the soft morning glory leaves. At the tippy-top, tendrils thrust up to the sky, twirling around some invisible support until, not finding it, they fall from their own weight. There are purple cone flowers that lean out over the rocks and dip to the grass. We plant amaranth seeds and soon see the red amaranth all over the Lower East Side, coming out of the cracks of sidewalks, flowerpots, rotting wood, over the top of a building, in empty lots. Our fast-growing mimosa tree drips delicate fernlike leaves; pink flowers like balls of cotton candy float on top like a boa, looking like the guy next door who tells me he is the one that leads the gay parade, right out in front with his feathers and diamonds. Sometimes the kids and I just lie in the grass, the grass that we seeded ourselves little by little, and we look up at the sky that we can now see in the space where the ailanthus used to be. We point at planes, name shapes in clouds. They turn somersaults, and I do, too. Their mother tells me she cries all night. She calls the police because the father stole her mother's jewelry, or this or that, but the police say there is nothing they can do. She says, "Now I have nothing left to steal. The apartment is empty, even the children's toys."

I say I will pray for her and her face lights up. She smiles.

"Oh, thank you, thank you," she says.

I know she thinks that because I am a Mennonite I have some way with praying, but I have no way. My mind just goes and goes down and down. I look inside for compassion, for sympathy, for hope, for some kindness and I can find not one bit, not even a tiny morsel.

My mother did not come to me after I asked her for forgiveness. Not yet.

As I pass 7A I see dogs watch eagerly for crumbs to fall from their owner's table, their heads darting down at imaginary treats then back up at their owner's eyes. This is how I wait.

The man who jumped off the roller coaster in my dream once brought a pine tree to my garden, but it was too big to transplant and he did not dig up enough of the roots. He called himself bipolar, said that lithium had saved his life, but still, when the manic high would come he would be off to the squat trying to keep it going, bending over his little blowtorch, mixing his baking soda and his little cocaine to make it last and last but it doesn't so that was the end of that.

We planted the bushy pine tree that he had dug up, I assumed, in a fit of optimism, but it turned brown right away. The lily of the valley he brought grew and so did the ferns. They are still growing now. If you want you can see for yourself on Eleventh Street between B and C, about halfway down the block.

They say, here, everything is going down. Either down or out. This is where a person you love can be burned in a little house they built on an empty lot on Avenue D and Ninth Street, where any number of people can disappear. We are all headed for Potter's Field down here on the Lower East Side, if we are lucky. Otherwise we may just overdose in some basement, or be beat up by a boyfriend and someone might leave us there so as not to have to call the police. There is something dead in the basement on the side of the building where the man in the storefront lives. When I come in the front door I hold a scarf over my mouth, run up the steps and try not to breathe. There are flies in the hall circling, and yellow strips full of them. To get to the lot I run through the flies, past the door where the smell is.

"Nasty," say the guys in the fake Jamaican restaurant next door. They are always smiling, even when they shake their heads and hold their noses.

It is Maundy Thursday at the Manhattan Mennonite Fellowship. I get down on my knees and wash feet and it is the minister's feet that I wash. We have had our disagreements so I am not surprised that I will be washing his feet. I sat on the other side of the room but the way it worked out, I had to carry the metal basin up to the front and put it down before the minister. I place the white fluffy towel on my lap, then put his feet there and dry his feet, then stand and kiss him on both cheeks. He reminds me of my mother, of the part of my mother I think might be inside of me, the part that I do not know how to make leave me, to kill, the part that makes living not something I want. I want him to disappear, too.

I suppose my mother felt the same way about me.

"You don't have to have it," the drummer says to me when we were friends in Arizona, "You can reconfigure." What he means is that I can rearrange my molecules, my DNA.

I died three times. The first time I was twenty-two, lying on a stretcher in a hallway of Colorado General Hospital Emergency Room with pneumonia, shivering in my down coat. I couldn't get my breath, couldn't breathe in, kept trying but panicked, thinking no one would see me in the hall. Then I felt so good, so happy, so free, so light, so warm, just floating above my body, watching the nurses wheel me down the hall and into a room, and, I thought, oh, man, I'm going to stay up here and never go down there again. Finally I am free of my mother, I thought. I have finally killed her, but then I remembered my daughter, and the second I did, I went back into my body.

I also spent many a ten-hour period at Bellevue Hospital Emergency Room with pneumonia, waiting to be seen, but one time I wanted to wait to go, trying to put off the hours of being there, under the fluorescent lights, in pain, ignored. I knew I should go, but I was so tired. I thought, I'll go in a little while. I was reading the Bible, Matthew, and came upon "Judge not, lest ye be judged," and those words jumped out, grabbed me and shook me until I knew I was dying, could see it, and I knew that my problem had been just that: being judgmental and self-righteous. Then I saw each thing I had done wrong in my life there before me like a movie, like a slow-motion movie. Each time I had lost my patience. Each time I had said hurtful words, had struck out. Hours and hours and more painful hours went by, with the torturously slow movie rolling and rolling and me crying, until, finally, it was over and I asked for forgiveness, then, for each thing that I had done wrong. Then I asked for help. The next thing I knew I was at Bellevue, where they saved my life, where someone in the basement found this problem with my DNA and gave me the medicine, this medicine that is saving my life.

It is New York that saved my life then and is saving my life now. I am being reconfigured, I am.

At night the drummer sits in a chair in the middle of a room and looks out over the canyon and travels, he says, to many places. I think he means outer space at the time, but now I think he meant much further out.

In the morning he walks past boulders, past yucca, past houses with seventy steps or ninety steps that go straight up to the doors. He walks to the town with no cars but he is not walking, he says. He does not believe in time or the regular kind of moving through space. He lives alone, miles down a canyon in a place that you would never find. It is on no road, no map, in between some boulders, hidden.

The thing he says I can change is a gene that is missing, a gene that tells most people's bodies to make a protein, the protein that I cannot live without and that I do not have. I do not need the medicine, he says.

The medicine is blood. There are procedures, IV bags and alcohol swabs. I put the needle in my vein. There are people that go to blood-buying businesses and they lie down and someone puts the needle in their arms and takes their blood and I know that it is very wrong but I put the needle in my vein and open up the tubing, watch the bag empty into my arm.

It is my good luck, this medicine.

Still, I know it is bad to take other people's blood. In the depressed upstate town where I live now the biggest building in the downtown says Blood Center. It is the only building in the downtown that is open, the others being all bordered up or empty and I see the thin people clutching their throats, or holding their arms, their heads darting this way and that, bent over, on their way there. I see them huddled outside, then I see them throw their cigarettes down and go in.

I should, I know, not be complicitous with exploitation. I should refuse the medicine and die like God apparently wants me to. But I already told you, I am not a good Mennonite. I want to be simple, but inside I am a mass of opposites, just like you, my bipolar ex-love, just like you.

The drummer is not talking about dying. What the drummer is talking about is reconfiguring.

"I am not up to it just yet," I say, "this reconfiguring," and he looks at me as if to say, well, then, aren't you in a pickle. I know he is right, I am.

Once I said the very same words to my sister, the one who is older, the one who is battered, who cowers. We are none of us good Mennonites, this branch of the Snyders that is called my family. We were walking in a museum and I was asking about the college class she had taken at the community college. She was telling me that her husband, who is from a desert place across the ocean, would not allow her to go to college anymore, that it was

forbidden.

"Leave him," I said.

"He will put a contract out on me," she said.

"Change your name, move to Oregon, go to college, " I said and offered her all my money, every penny I had.

"I really am used to the money," my sister said. And I said it. I used the word pickle. It is something I will have to get down on my knees about in the future, or perhaps right now.

There were other things I could have done. Now I know I should have gone to help her pack her clothes, made arrangements for the plane, driven us to the airport, boarded the plane and flown with her to Oregon, stayed on and helped her find an apartment, the library, the community college.

I, too, have known terror, have been held up on a wall and punched, had my share of black eyes, broken noses, have been trapped with no way out.

I know the computer, the one on which I am typing this right now, works by saying no or yes, that so much infinity can be from just no and yes, but no is so hard, takes so much more than what I can bear. I can say no, but the part of me that is my mother comes up, takes over and that I cannot bear. There is so much inside to reconfigure. Little by little, I tell myself, little by little.

Once, in Guatemala, I asked someone from Belize how the people of Belize got along with the Mennonites there. "Good. They grow all the food," he said, "And if anyone wants something they have, the Mennonites just stand aside and let them have it."

In Ohio in the 1960s, someone escaped from prison and killed a police officer and continued running. He ran to a Mennonite farm, where the door was opened for him. He killed the entire family, which put up no fight, then went on his way and was eventually caught. The Mennonite and Amish of the community got in their buggies and made the long trip to the governor's mansion, where they camped out, pleading for mercy for the murderer.

The drummer was a point man in Vietnam. Once, he said, he was on the top of a mountain with his battalion and he was looking through binoculars which were on a tripod, doing reconnaissance.

"When you do that," he said, "you have to have someone spot you."

"Spot you?" I said.

"When you are looking through the binoculars, you are vulnerable. You cannot use your gun. Someone has to watch out for you."

What happened, he said, is that they were pelted with what he called enemy fire. He said it got everything; everyone was dead; even the tripod legs were hit and the tripod fell over. "And I," he said, "reconfigured." He splayed his fingers out, thrusting his arms up. "My molecules all expanded, dissipated out in the air so the bullets could pass through, and then they came back together. I was the only one not hit."

But he was wrong because there was shrapnel in his leg that had gone through his boot and, thirty-four years later, he fell and his leg was trapped and part of the shrapnel got loose and went to his brain and killed him, which was when he came to visit me while I was sitting on my floor in New York City.

"Why didn't you reconfigure?" I asked, but he didn't answer. I heard later he refused medical treatment.

My next-door neighbor, the one who leads the gay parade with his boas and flowers, the one who planted a Chinese maple on his side and handed me a spray nozzle for the hose over the fence, is sick. He is so thin, so thin, but we do not talk of that. Instead we talk of annuals, biannuals, bulbs and seeds. He tells me what I should do about the gladioli. On the other side of his fence is the garden of the woman who lives in the empty boarded-up building. The one in the babushka and galoshes that gets her water from the fire hydrant. She plants stuffed animals in her lot. She pulls out the part of them where there would be a penis or a vagina and hangs them by the neck on the fence with wire. She puts a pan over their heads or sometimes she pulls the heads off, too. She has naked mannequins, dirty dolls, American flags, and Christmas decorations, all mutilated.

At church camp, at Camp Zion, I would sit on the hill for vespers. I was happy, so happy with the light changing, the trees changing from green to black, the sky from blue to orange or pink, then navy with first one star, then another, and us singing about God coming by, about letting it begin with me. This is my story, this is my song. It is a gift to be simple, a gift to be free. I could have lived at Camp Zion forever and ever: tables piled high with food, the swimming hole, the cabins, the baseball games, the yearly hike to the strip mines with miles of shale like the surface of the moon, with deep pools of bright green or bright orange and someone asking me what I thought God was. Where is God, they asked.

My landlady tells me that she has cancer. "Oh," I say and hug her, crying, "Don't leave me." I say. Then she looks at the garden and smiles holding her arms across her stomach. She says, "You have made this a real estate." She laughs at her joke. "Imagine me with a real estate," she says. She brings out a hose so I can water.

The children have lost interest in the garden. The oldest girl wants to be a dancer. She shows me moves she learns at school: salsa, merengue. She wants to teach me. She takes my hand.

"What a good dancer you are," I say, "You are so fast." She has a Hello Kitty backpack and a Powder Puff shirt. I wonder if she has been safe. There are so many crack thin men that come and go, that sleep in the hall, the basement.

The littlest girl says to me, "Your eyes are like stars." The boy runs after her, grabs her dress and pulls her down. He takes a stick and pushes it through the huge leaves of the comfrey plant. I take his arm.

"It is a living thing," I say, and he looks at me like I am so stupid, that of course he knows that the plant is a living thing. Don't I see that that is precisely the point he is trying to make? He looks at me like he will push the stick through me if I don't shut up right now. He holds it up threateningly, pushes his jaw forward, his chest forward, does not blink, holds it over my head. I am down on my knees and look at him, this beautiful living thing in the beautiful garden. His eyes so luminous. His lashes so long. The light is streaming through the morning glories behind him. He brings the stick down beside me. It breaks on the stone. He takes the piece that is left and goes back to hitting the plant. The plant will only grow stronger, bigger, with more branches.

Just like all of us.

On the way to bury my mother's ashes, I hold the box while my sister drives her Mercedes. As I carry the box up the hill to the gravesite we bought next to the graves of my mother's mother and father, I hear my mother speaking to me. "Oh," she says, "I did not know you were going to bring me here." Her voice sounds like a young girl's voice, giddy in a way I never heard my mother's voice. It is a beautiful spot with huge spruce and oak, green grass, and weeping willows.

"This is very good," my mother says, "I am so happy about this." Her voice is more and more excited the closer we come to the spot. I think it is funny she is speaking to me, her least favorite. I look to my sister and brother to see if they hear her voice, but they give me no indication. My sister has made a bag out of cloth to put my mother's ashes in and she asks the gravediggers, who are standing by, if they have a knife to open the cardboard box. They slouch over, looking very much like the people who sell their blood in depressed towns all over the country, those people who save my life, and the one with long, blond hair pulls out a pocketknife and starts to open the box. It is not easy. There are several cardboard boxes all very securely taped shut. Finally we find the plastic box.

"My mother will not be buried in plastic," my sister says and she holds open the cloth bag that she had quilted while the gravediggers pour the ashes out of the plastic box.

While they are pouring, I say to my mother, "If you are going to be talking to me, why don't you do something for me? Show me where you are." Immediately, or faster then any immediately could ever be, I see the grass, the trees, the stones, the dirt all vibrating, the bright colors iridescent, vibrant beyond the natural.

"Okay," I say, "That's enough," and everything returns back to how it was. Then my sister leaves, and I follow my brother to his car. We drive to the downtown of the place where we grew up, which is like the downtown of the place I am living now, all boarded up except for the Blood Center. Nothing is like it had been when I would walk downtown after school and go to the big stone library, or to the candy store, or Woolworth's, or the big department store. The big magnificent buildings made of stone with angels flying on the corners or women draped in stone dresses are all empty. We circle around these old buildings, my brother and I, until we see a pool hall open and we climb the stairs to the huge deserted space with wooden floors and we play pool all afternoon.

I tell him what happened when we were pouring ashes and that is when he tells me about how he had felt her before he saw our mother passing in the hearse.

My brother works for the man that batters my sister. "Keep him away from your daughter," I say, and he says, yes he knows. "There are so many more bad things there. I cannot say all of them," he says. He does not want to work for my brother-in-law but he does not know how to get away, he says. "We are all of us complicitous in so many things, so much bad," he says. Of this, I am sure. No matter how much I dig in my lot, no matter how many stones I throw away, there are always more and more.

If there is a murder done by the state, some capital punishment, Mennonites are required to stand outside to show that they are not complicitous, but we all are. If there is murder done by war we are required to stand in the line of fire if we can, or march or object, to resist. There is a man from the Manhattan Mennonite Fellowship who has walked the line of fire in Iraq since before the first Desert Storm. He learns where there will be bombing, then goes there and alerts the Council of Churches that he is there. The United States cannot bomb in a place where there is a U.S. citizen. While so many have gone to Iraq and died, he is still alive after almost twenty years, being shielded by families, respected by all.

"I cry every night," the mother says, but still every day she walks the children in their uniforms to the Catholic school, the private school. She is so small, so delicate, so straight and proud walking with her children in the community, down her street.

"I do not know if God will answer my prayers," she says, "It is not for me to know, but I am thinking that maybe not. I cannot know why." She is crying. I ask if she has relatives somewhere, someone who would take her in. She shakes her head. "Who wants a mother and three children?" she says.

My friend, the one who was burned up in his little house on his lot, said that once he was taken up to the projects, to an empty apartment, accused of being a snitch and then he heard the plastic being pulled behind him. He said it was only his charm that saved him.

"What did you say?" I asked.

"That I was no snitch. That they been knowing me since I was a kid. They know my mom, my dad." Still, eventually he is dead, his body burned with his little house, the house where, he said, if you looked out the window, you looked into the next lot, as though you were in Kansas. Now he is gone, some say murdered; the fire was a cover. So much beauty in one soul, my beautiful friend, who used to glide by on his skateboard, with his black and white little dog pulling him along.

But then a big company buys the building, offers the mother of the children money to move. "God comes in different clothes," she says, and soon we are all out on the sidewalk and they are getting into a van, saying good-bye. The oldest girl, now up to my shoulder, is wearing a sweater with fake fur on it and swinging her Barbie backpack. "Little by little," she says, "Maybe if you try, you could leave, too."

"Little by little," I say.

I call the drummer's daughter, to say I am sorry for her loss. She says her father was too good for this world and I agree.

As for me I think I will be here for a while. I am right where I belong, down on my knees, clearing debris out of the dirt of my lot, on the street they call Little Nam.

KATHERINE ARNOLDI has been awarded the Henfield Trans-atlantic Fiction Award, the DeJur Award, the New York Foundation of the Arts Award in Fiction, and the Newhouse Award. Her graphic novel, *The Amazing True Story of a Teenage Single Mom* (Hyperion, 1998), received the New York Foundation of the Arts Award in Drawing and two American Library Awards, was nominated for a Will Eisner Award in the Graphic Novel, and was named one of the Top Ten Books of the Year by *Entertainment Weekly*. In 2006 she started the Katherine Arnoldi Scholarship Fund for Teenage Mothers. Her website, www.katherinearnoldi.com, has a Guide for Colleges for Pregnant and Parenting Students. She lives in New York City and is in a doctoral program in creative writing at Binghamton University.

The Juniper
Prize

This volume is the second recipient of the Juniper Prize
for Fiction, established in 2004 by the University of
Massachusetts Press in collaboration with the UMass
Amherst MFA Program for Poets and Writers, to be
presented annually for an outstanding work of literary
fiction. Like its sister award, the Juniper Prize for Poetry
established in 1976, the prize is named in honor of
Robert Francis (1901–1987), who lived for many years
at Fort Juniper, Amherst, Massachusetts.